NATURAL SELECTION

■ **Margaret Mulvihill** was born and brought up in Ireland. She studied history at University College Dublin and at Birkbeck College in London, and has worked mainly as a history editor and writer. She lives in south London with a film-maker and their daughter. **Natural Selection** is her first novel.

PANDORA PRESS FICTION ORIGINAL

NATURAL SELECTION

Margaret Mulvihill

Aithníonn ciaróg ciaróg eile

Irish proverb: one black beetle will
know another

PANDORA

LONDON, BOSTON AND HENLEY

First published in 1985
by Pandora Press (Routledge & Kegan Paul plc)
14 Leicester Square, London WC2H 7PH, England

9 Park Street, Boston, Mass. 02108, USA and

Broadway House, Newtown Road,
Henley on Thames, Oxon RG9 1EN, England

Set in Sabon 10 on 13 point
by Fontwise
and printed in Great Britain
by The Guernsey Press Co. Ltd,
Guernsey, Channel Islands

Library of Congress Cataloging in Publication Data

Mulvihill, Margaret.
Natural selection.

I. Title.
PR6063.U466N3   1985   823'.914
British Library CIP data also available

ISBN 0–86358–064–5 (c)
0–86358–058–0 (p)

For Mick and Katrina

CHAPTER ONE

———————— ✳ ————————

Like a desperate wasp clambering up the sides of a sticky jam jar, Maureen Ryan struggled out of a dream whose details were by now familiar.

In this unwelcome dream she had been in her granny's house, frantically searching for some boiled sucking sweets that she knew were hidden away somewhere upstairs. But when she walked into the big upstairs bedroom she found a man and a woman asleep in the bed. They looked beautiful and peaceful lying together: their arms were entwined and their faces were almost touching, like the glycerine couples in advertisements for luxury bed linen. They were Martin and Laura Kershaw. Very slowly Laura opened her large eyes and for a few cold moments she gazed calmly at the intruder. Then she told her to go back to bed, as if Maureen were a peevish, sleepless child.

The desolate, primal atmosphere of this dream, which she had been having regularly during the previous weeks, hung over Maureen as she began to focus on her real surroundings, a rather dark bedroom in a house of the same vintage as her grandmother's. She guessed that her flatmate must have woken her because there was a mug of tea on the bedside table. She sat up, holding the warm mug in both of her hands, and her first timid sip told her that, in keeping with one of his many principles, Fabian had refused to put sugar in it. But though unable to orchestrate pleasant sleep dreams, Maureen was prepared for such contingencies as sugar-less tea. A deft grope beneath the bed yielded a wrapped sugar cube and as she stirred the solution with a pencil she was able to dispel some of the poignancy of her dream with grumpy thoughts about Fabian's puritanism.

Eventually, she managed to wrench herself from the bed and down to the bathroom. There she continued an ill-advised battle against intermittently bleeding gums and scrubbed against a body that she felt particularly ambiguous about on this Monday morning. Then she set about assembling an outfit worthy of a publisher's editorial trainee.

All the ingredients for such a role were there. They had been culled mainly from the street markets and junk shops she visited on Saturdays, but clothes-wise Maureen rarely had the courage to match her imagination and as a consultant on her physical image Fabian was no great help. So it was only after a great deal of wasted deliberation that she settled on a soft cream blouse, which, with its delicate pearl buttons, was incongruously virginal with the khaki jeans that went underneath.

Her face was long and, at this time of year, only slightly freckled. Most of the time it was hidden behind a cascade of lightly permed dark brown hair and it had a paradoxical way of acquiring an interestingly consumptive pallor *only* when Maureen was feeling well and healthy. Her mother often said that she would age with dignity on account of her wide shoulders (which would hold tweed suits well) but in general Maureen was disappointed by evolution's failure to meet the metropolitan challenge on her behalf.

She *was* fashionably thin but her correspondingly wide hips made her *feel* large and cumbersome so she slouched in order to hide a non-existent bulk. But Maureen was also an optimist and this negative body image did not stop her from entertaining a hope that she would rise one day as a long-nosed, gloriously photogenic beauty. Because of this optimism she was more disillusioned than disgusted when she stared into the foxed mirror above her dressing table and prodded a painfully latent spot on her chin. Maybe, hopefully, it was a premenstrual spot.

Looking like an Edwardian gentleman in an anachronistically small kitchen, Fabian Kemp was reading a newspaper as he dipped toast into a perfectly opened soft-boiled egg. He glanced benignly at Maureen and wished her a good day as she seized a banana and found a plastic carrier bag for the proofs she had indexed that weekend.

Down the street, with the instinctive urgency of a migrating rat, Maureen rushed to work. She passed the massive Greek woman on her way to a steamy day of toil at the launderette and the mournful queue waiting outside the doctor's surgery for the shrinking services of the welfare state. As she crossed over to the Tube station she met the old woman with the still discernible Cork accent who regularly solicited passers-by for cigarettes. This gaunt lady held her handbag like a royal, both of her hands clutching its strap above thin knees, and by now Maureen knew that she should simply say that she did not smoke. The Corkwoman accepted this response with polite grace, but Maureen had seen her back away angrily from offers of money.

The station newsagent offered her newspaper with a cheery servility and she took it from him silently. She clutched hard at the 'quality' daily that simply symbolized an effort to connect with reality (she rarely read it), blackening her hands, and ultimately her painful chin, in the process. When a train came, it was crowded, so she had to stand.

Facing Maureen was a stout woman holding the lead of a small black mongrel dog. This skinny little animal was nervously thrusting its wet snout up under the reassuring skirts of its owner, who kept pushing it away with an air of frantic composure. Maureen smiled at this scene but averted her eyes when the man beside her also registered amusement and manoeuvred her bulky carrier bag as a device to keep him out of the space that she needed for her morning reverie.

She started to confront a major preoccupation. It was now the penultimate day upon which it might be reasonable for Martin Kershaw to ring her up and enquire about the progress of the index. If he did not ring up, it would be equally reasonable to suppose not only that he had no special interest in their working relationship, but also that their having slept together once was of no ongoing significance. Maureen was trying very hard to be reasonable. When the train belched into a mysterious halt and some of its entombed passengers were sending up ritualistic cluckings of disgust, she started to lull herself away from distressing thoughts about Martin by bringing on the comforting order of well-rehearsed daydreams.

First, like a careful video cassette consumer, she flicked through her selection of old favourites, which was fed by such adolescent reading matter as *The Scarlet Pimpernel* and *Quo Vadis*. These innocent constructs – nothing was consummated in her repertoire – had carried Maureen through the vicissitudes of puppy fat and acne, and now they served her during a more complex trough.

She summoned up a favourite sequence in which she was a duochrome princess: that is, a woman with perfectly red, or black, hair and brown, or ivory, skin (these details took a pleasant time to resolve). Captured by a Roman centurion whose golden thighs beneath his Latin textbook tunic were inspired by memories of Charlton Heston in *Ben Hur*, she was to eventually persuade him of her nobility, and make him fall passionately in love with her. This special noble quality of Maureen's could have no immediate material basis, since, of course, all her jewels and precious ornaments would have been confiscated during the ransacking of her ancestral palace. It would become evident from her regal bearing, her *mien* and an ability to play various musical instruments mesmerizingly.

On this day Maureen jumped a reel and went on to the climactic scene where the once-lecherous but now chastened Roman was gratefully accepting a healing tribal potion from her on his sickbed. She dwelled on this delicious moment until the train pulled in at Leicester Square. Reality drew closer to her as she saw, ahead of her on the escalator, Roger Andrews, the senior editor. His round bottom protruded through the back slit of the trenchcoat that he wore in an attempt to look like a political journalist.

New Vision, where Maureen worked, was one of the newer publishing houses, a commercial and therefore enduring fruit of the cultural upheavals of the late 1960s. It was a company catering for the masses with 'highly illustrated' books about health, gardening, interior decorating, cooking and natural history. One year books about herbs might do very well, and the next year it might be babycare. New Vision prided itself on being able to do the equivalent of selling fridges to Eskimos, selling books on mountain-climbing to the Dutch, for example.

This was New Vision's year of the swamp. Already, *Swamp Animals*, *Birds of the Swamp*, *Insects of the Swamp* and even *Peoples of the Swamp* (which featured many colour photographs of nude but acceptably primitive females) had been unleashed upon the world, and Maureen was working on an amalgam of all these provisionally entitled *The World of Swamps*. She had arrived in London one year previously on the strength of a subsidized journey to an interview for a job that she had not got. Instead she had found work as a temporary typist and it had been in this capacity that she had first wormed her way into New Vision.

She sat at a corner desk in an open-plan office painted Covent Garden green. The plants that crowded out the room were watered once a week by a cooing colleague (usually Laura) and once a month they also received the specialist attentions of an entrepreneurial hippy. When a plant died and had to be taken away with an undertaker's delicacy of feeling by this green man, Maureen felt relieved. It had been explained to her that the plants helped to purify the air, but her attitude remained negative, like that of the Elizabethans towards the contagion of the night.

In her crepuscular corner Maureen was sometimes able to think unprofitable thoughts without being observed. She was espcially fond of perusing the list that she kept in her desk's top drawer. She had begun making these lists when she had started going to weekly confession after reaching the age of seven – the Thomistic age of reason. She had felt a need to present the priest with a rattle of plausible venial sins and so she noted any errors that she *could have* committed in order to provide her confessor with some forgiving satisfaction. Fifteen years later, however, it was not sins that she listed but items that she thought she should buy or save for, books she felt she ought to read and words like 'atavistic' or 'hermeneutic' that needed repeated looking up before she could use them confidently.

The items listed under these basic self-improving categories were continually being revised, amended and even rejected. For example, her last working lunch with Martin had persuaded Maureen that she ought to read James Joyce's *Ulysses*. She did not think that she could continue in any comfort to nod in pseudo-informed amusement at his references to it, and since he and many other representatives of the British intelligentsia derived most of their knowledge of her country from this single source, it was obligatory reading.

Another favourite theme of Martin's was her Catholicism. 'If you can't be Jewish,' he once said, 'the next best thing is Irish Catholic.' Of plain-speaking Methodist stock himself, he claimed to envy the medieval coherence of Maureen's formation and presumed, correctly, that she was suffused with guilt. Because she did not want to dent any of Martin's illusions about her, Maureen did not tell him that in this she was not manifesting the symptoms of a Catholic girlhood so much as the inevitable anxieties of any young person desperately trying to honour the aspirations of lower middle-class parents.

Maureen saved up witty thoughts for Martin and sometimes wasted them by blurting them out at the wrong moment. It seemed to her that she and Martin made love verbally and she wondered if there was some Freudian term for such substitutionism, the artful aphorism in place of a caress, for they had only been physically intimate once. She often felt inclined to take some rudely sensual initiative, but she did not dare because she was not certain of the chemistry between them. It was just possible that he preferred things the way they usually were.

By ten o'clock, as newspapers were put away and diaries were checked, the Swamp department had settled down to work. Maureen cleaned her spectacles and began to erase some of the comments that were pencilled-in on the typescript before her.

The World of Swamps had been written by a poor would-be novelist who had retired, somewhat prematurely, with a hackly set of tools dominated by a complete *Encyclopaedia Britannica*, to north Wales. Parts of his typescript were now so calloused with liquid white-out that they had the texture of a Braille script. At the end of a day pushing around it Maureen was tattooed with all the colours on offer from New Vision's stationery cupboard. Her work was often as tedious as it was badly paid, but she appreciated the fact that it was respectable. Mindful of the enormous reserve army behind them, and of their luck in ducking real 'trade', Maureen and most of the other young arts graduates who made up the bulk of New Vision's workforce dared not ask for more money.

Stanley H. Ruckster had started New Vision a decade or so earlier. Because he was bald he looked older than forty-five, but he was fanatically fit and he had been known to refuse pay rises to persistent smokers. He had a habit of thrusting his tongue into the mouths of young graduate geishas who ventured too near him at office dos, but he did not take advantage of his publisher's seigneurial license beyond this. Despite the fact that his employees addressed him by his first name, Stanley ran New Vision with feudal confidence. At the Christmas beano his staff gazed in greedy awe at great dishes of cold meats and taramosalata, and the personnel manager had no difficulty in leading the jovial chorus that followed his jocular asides.

Stanley's county life-style demonstrated the accommo-dating vigour of Britain's *ancien régime*. An only child of Polish immigrant parents, he had been reared in Worthing and he had never been to university. But, like the brilliant woman who also needs to be thought beautiful, he rode horses and sent his children, Titania and Minos, to the most prestigious public schools. He lived with his wife (a fragile and elegant creature whose family had once been useful to him) in a large house in Buckinghamshire.

Right now Stanley was conferring with Laura Kershaw (wife of Maureen's Martin) and Roger Andrews in the Swamp room. He was wearing a tracksuit because outside New Vision's front entrance a chauffeur was sitting in the car that would take him to Hyde Park, where he jogged each morning. Gently, he rebuked Laura for having had too fastidious a policy towards a swamp author's clichés.

Laura nodded smilingly at his comments: she was still learning how to cater for the general reader. Her ash-blonde hair was touchingly tired-looking this morning and she had it pulled into a knot at the back of her small head.

Roger kept trying to look busy even as he was listening to Stanley and eventually this, and his cigarette, irritated the *padrone* enough to send him away. But even as Laura smiled she was aware of Maureen's cold stare from her dark corner. She knew that Maureen resented her successful collusion with Stanley and Roger, but she did not know that this resentment extended to the hold that she had over her husband.

Laura's erring husband was the managing editor of *Aspidistra*, a literary journal with a small circulation and great, if declining, prestige – Maureen had even heard of it in Dublin. Martin Kershaw had a certain eminence because of his administrative centrality among a group of leading intellectuals, who were occasionally induced to sell their souls as the writers of forewords and introductions to New Vision's products.

Stanley had first met Laura at a book launch when she had been a depressed and bored librarian. She had immediately impressed him, not least on account of the remarkable Pre-Raphaelite shadows under her eyes, and he had felt soothed by her demanding, undeniable femininity. Laura had asked him sensitive questions about his enterprise without presuming any answers. With one small hand pushing the neat Victorian brow and her pink and attractively bruised-looking lips pursed in a considerately reflective way, she was a vision of oracular womanhood.

Stanley had suggested that she should come and see him about alternative work. When, to his surprise, she did, he had offered her a place at New Vision as an editor. Laura's inexperience made her the object of some 'craft' resentment at first, and Roger had even christened her 'Stanley's bellibone'. This nickname never travelled beyond the rooms equipped with dictionaries, however, and when everyone was sure that she was not having an affair with Stanley and she had proved herself to be a conscientious worker, Laura earned acceptance. Even Roger was won over by the serious but sympathetic dimension that she lent to everyday operations.

Once Stanley had departed for his jog, Laura and Roger walked over to Vanessa, the fourth occupant of the Swamp room whose secretarial function was sculpturally marked by the skeletal chair that she sat on and the large typewriter dominating her desk surface. Roger muttered and spilled cigarette ash on her as he was handing over bits of paper and she was setting up her machine in order to type Stanley's comments.

Like a reluctant *Flintstones* animal-machine, Vanessa allowed herself to be the intermediary between the Swamp Department and the outside world. She answered the telephones and deciphered Roger's handwriting, but she had a dignified, strictly functional attitude to her work. Maureen chose to interpret Vanessa's coolness as a principled response to Roger's odiousness, but alas it was more complicated than that. In fact Vanessa resented both her young colleagues equally. As far as she was concerned they were more alike than they were different: Roger as he pronounced upon the nation's woes, sneering at her *Daily Mail* while trying to catch its headline; Maureen as she sought some mysterious solidarity, clamouring indecently about menstruation and other aspects of life that Vanessa still liked to consider private. It was particularly galling that Maureen had done well out of the fact that she was no good at doing what Vanessa did. She was barely able to type in fact and they had made her a junior editor because once installed at New Vision she had been very hard to shift.

Vanessa had been organizing her mealticket since she was seventeen and now, among graduate contemporaries, she was the only truly literate person in the Swamp department. She could spell and she was confident with semi-colons, while they had to re-learn all that after years of self-indulgence at university. Only Laura was exempt from Vanessa's disapproval, and that was because she was older and more considerate, a latecomer to the world. To Laura Vanessa confided her unease about the future, for it was obvious that Roger Andrews was not the sort of upwardly mobile man in symbiosis with whom she could hope to raise herself as a 'personal assistant'. Laura had helped Vanessa with her forms and sent her off to do an 'A' level. If bits of paper from academic institutions gave them the right to boss her around, Vanessa was determined to get some for herself.

CHAPTER TWO

—————————— ❖ ——————————

Some days later, in a third-floor flat in Crouch End, Martin Kershaw was lighting the fifteenth cigarette he had started (he never finished a cigarette) that morning. He wanted to scream because he could not settle down to his work. He wanted to stop thinking about the tumultous cistern and the Easter weekend. It always seemed that just when he was about to capture on paper something that had been fecklessly and intermittently gestating Laura made claims upon him. He thought it so unfair. There is nothing intrinsically sexist about the creative dilemma, but his wife made it into another aspect of the male arsenal against her concern with the pastel details of everyday life. Laura seemed determined to resist analytical conversations, the newspapers and his need to place things.

When Martin was bored with Laura he thought that she was too agnostic, even bovine in her serene immunity to any kind of commitment. She never expressed a dislike for people, although she sometimes found individuals too arrogant, too dull or simply difficult. She was capable of being vegetarian for one week and a ravenous carnivore for the next, and when she was ill, which was rare, she retired to bed to emerge, a day later, rested and completely recuperated. Not for her sudden weight gain or loss, mysterious headaches or deteriorating eyesight. She moved through life as if she had been sent there as an observer, whereas Maureen Ryan, with her rushed judgments and polemical prejudices, acted as if she were an exile. On an impulse he was later to regret, Martin resolved to ring her up.

Martin's official connection with Maureen had stemmed from Laura's guilt. She had felt a need to conciliate her junior at work because of the unsolicited privileges Stanley bestowed upon her, so she had suggested Maureen as a likely indexer for a collection of historic articles from *Aspidistra*, which were due for publication in book form as an anthology.

Maureen seized the ringing phone with too much alacrity and one moment after she had put it down, she regretted her over-enthusiastic agreement to lunch with Martin on that very day.

Since the weekend her breasts had felt a little more heavy. It was not too late to be optimistic about the imminence of her period, but horrible doubts preyed upon her. Did they often feel this way? Was she imagining that her discomfort was a familiar herald of the monthly purge? One thing was certain — she could not confide in Martin if the fleeting anxiety that crept up on her unawares was justified. At least she was sure about what she should do. There was no question of becoming a mother while more worldly aspirations remained unasserted. These forebodings added a certain testiness to her anticipation of Martin.

They usually met in a pub of her choice in Soho. She deliberately never went there on any other pretext because she wanted to maintain its purity of association. The Greyhound was presided over by a grumpy landlord, whose customers derived a masochistic satisfaction from his apparent disapproval of their purpose in being there. Under his hostile gaze, Maureen carried two pints to the darkest corner. Martin was always late.

Tudor roses adhered to the pillars around the central bar and a portrait of Oscar Wilde flanked one of the cash registers. The walls were covered with Victorian hunting scenes and the windows were framed by thickly-bunched white nylon curtains. A cowboy-saloon-style swing door led to a Regency-pink Ladies Room and in every alcove there were brass horse shoes and nautical instruments.

Seeing Martin, Maureen immediately pretended to be engrossed in her newspaper.

'Hi,' he sighed affectionately, noticing that for all her apparent concentration Maureen was not wearing her glasses. 'Sorry I'm late. I bumped into your flatmate's stepfather on the way here and he reminded me of the party this weekend. Are you going?'

'I don't know yet.' Although this was perfectly true, Maureen's non-commital answer did not mean that she was considering the party as just another option that weekend: it was the first she had heard of it. She resolved to quiz Fabian as soon as she got home. Meanwhile, she gestured extravagantly at the pub décor and declared that she had enjoyed her wait because of the 'eclectic generosity' of the person responsible for the pub's competing ambiences. She felt pleased with her expression of this complex observation, but was a little let down by Martin's response. He simply glanced around the pub before taking the first sip of his pint.

She began to explain some of the difficulties she had had with the index to Martin – problems to do with Chinese names and pseudonyms – and it only took about ten minutes for them to sort out these queries. Then she began to feel desperate in case he would leave early, especially since she knew that with Laura's connivance she could have a longer lunch 'hour' than usual. She tried to avoid looking too lingeringly at Martin. If she looked into his face it was as if his lips, the mouth that she wanted to cover, was moving teasingly towards her. She suspected that when he smiled it was with a certain cruelty, as if he enjoyed gazing into her desirous soul.

When she was very young Maureen had often tried to
elect cabbage and boiled eggs as her favourite foods
because there was no tension in their pursuit, not like
breast of chicken or apple pie after which there was a
universal race. She also schooled herself into liking the
hard chocolates that nobody else craved and now she was
angry with herself for wanting Martin because, with his
blunt, roguish features, his boyishly thick black hair and
the long angularity of his build, he was too obviously
desirable. It seemed to her that all women wanted to
nurture Martin, so why had she joined the hopeless,
clamouring throng?

After about thirty minutes Maureen and Martin found
themselves locked into an impasse that had arisen in
several previous conversations. Because of her annoyance
with herself, her anxiety about the possible consequences
of their love-making and her resentment of what she
suspected was a studied neutrality with her, Maureen
began to be rattled by Martin's complacent espousal of
what she referred to as the 'new rugged individualism'.

Maureen wanted to be a woman of qualities like Laura.
She wanted to be somebody or to do something, but she
did not know who she should become or what she should
try to do. It was difficult in London – a metropolitan
density of talent and ambition – where she felt that, for a
start, her flat and ordinary name was a handicap. It was
okay for the likes of Laura, so calm and beautiful, to be an
editor, the little woman behind every great author (even
though none of the latter roamed New Vision's premises)
because Laura Kershaw was already special.

Poor Maureen had her small nose pressed up against the
cold window fronting a bewildering display of desirable
things. Most of the time she was too paralysed by an
omnivorous greed to enter, but the longer she stayed
outside, the more the shop kept changing its wares. Right
now she craved the kind of respectability that would give

her access to the world Martin belonged to. But what would be her best buy to that end?

Martin was troubled by his companion's intensity. He listened patiently while she moaned about New Vision and then said, 'Look at Fabian. He's deliberately avoided using his connections to get on. If he went round to Clive and Dolores for lunch every Sunday he'd have his photographs all over the place in no time. You're condescending about him because you think he's not clued up enough, and at other times you accuse him of having a great big silver spoon stuck in his gob.'

'He's not on his own. Dolores bought him the flat and he could afford to be unemployed for six months if he wanted to figure something out. He can have cheap holidays in innumerable country cottages any time he likes.' Maureen instantly regretted her last remark because its pettiness undermined her retaliation.

'But he doesn't,' was Martin's grim rejoinder.

'Oh, you deliberately choose to misinterpret me,' she said angrily.

Martin was thinking that if Maureen wanted to be better understood she should express herself more precisely. She was exhausting him by demanding a sophisticated empathy with her frustrations. He sensed something else, something more than a simple lust, behind her interest in him. But because his own ego was far from stable Martin failed to appreciate his status in Maureen's eyes as a fluent dropper of famous names.

'The point is,' Maureen continued, 'that if you are already somebody, then you become beautiful or clever or chic. If you have any greatness by association you get more heaped at you. Fabian is just like a young knight being sent out on his quest in the knowledge that he will return one day to his inheritance.' After this she began to feel very emotional indeed, almost tearful.

Feeling at a loss, Martin walked over to the bar and

bought them each a brandy. Then, hoping to revive her good humour, he told her that she was beautiful.

'I suppose that's got to be good enough for a woman,' she grinned sarcastically, and he looked at her and reminded himself that she was only about twenty-four years old. At the same time he had a prickly memory of the reference that Laura's illustrious godfather had supplied for his first job. Martin began to think more kindly of his wife.

'It's two o'clock,' he said, 'we'd better move.'

But Maureen could not bear to go back to her office just yet, so she spent some more time buying very small amounts of various foods in an Italian shop. This reassured her because the more innards and olives she ate, and the more beans that filled her kitchen jars, the more confidently bourgeois she felt. Fabian had gently initiated her into these tastes and as she stood behind a film producer in the queue, she was grateful for his humane interest in her and sorry for having so churlishly bitten the hand that was feeding her.

Laura Kershaw walked briskly out of the New Vision building. She was heading for the swimming baths where, once or twice a week, she went through a strenuous purification rite. Today she attracted the attention of other pedestrians as she spoke to herself and caught her breath in irritated memory of the previous evening. Martin's temporality eluded her. That morning he had seemed remote and abstracted and, yet, the night before he had been veering on the sentimental, forcing her to recall moments in their past with a mindless nostalgia. She was absorbed in defining her presence at New Vision while he was running morbidly along some other track.

Having got down in the water, Laura struggled up and down the pool for a couple of lengths. The holiness of this ritual, its combination of intimacy with anonymity, appealed to her. Of the worldly identities of the almost naked swimmers with wet, flattened hair little was obvious except, of course, their sex, and the rude democracy of the pool took account of this division.

Like big hard tanks, the men ploughed up and down regardless of human obstacles in their paths and at first Laura, like most of the other women, kept decorously to the sides with a gentle breaststroke. Gradually, however, as a blissful uterine oblivion of time, effort and mind came over her, she became able to move more smoothly and easily through the water. Then, glorying in her transition from a peripheral, panting exertion, she struck boldly down the pool's middle with a strong swathe of her own. When she emerged Laura felt pliant and pleasurably tamed by the exercise. She remained sure that Martin was intolerably egotistical and that she was intolerably tolerant, but he still touched a chord in her.

As she walked back to New Vision Laura thought a little more fondly about the way in which her marriage staggered through compromises, and of the good times when their moods were complementary, the early days especially, when they had both lived out equal, exampunctuated lives. Even so, she had always scorned her mother's unromantically minimal rapport with her father and now she was beginning to question the nobility of her own compromise.

At two forty-five Maureen arrived back. Vanessa glanced up as she passed and then continued to study the classified pages in the magazine which had been thrust upon her that morning at the Tube exit. Roger's return was acknowledged when she put it in her bin and selected some carbon paper. Soon they had all settled back to work, if the continuation of Roger and Maureen's arguments about 'humankind' versus 'mankind' could have been regarded as such.

Turning away from them, Vanessa began to type. When she felt especially provoked she drove hard on her electric machine's underliner, which gave off a rattle like that of a machine gun. Occasionally she picked up a telephone to tell some unemployed proofreader that Mr Andrews was still in a meeting and every now and then she benevolently eyed her futurist shoes. Defiantly, these fragile cathedrals of wood and pearlized leather encased Vanessa's feet. They had provoked Maureen's indignant censure as she recalled the bound feet of pre-revolutionary Chinese women and worried about how Vanessa might flee from would-be rapists, but Roger had intervened to say that she could stab them with the spiky heels.

At four o'clock Roger said that 'coffee would be nice'. Knowing the significance of this habitual declaration, Vanessa duly slinked towards a greasy table supporting a collection of Neolithic pottery mugs and a wet bag of sugar. This would be the last cup to keep them awake until the end of the working day.

Still a little fuddled by lunch-time wine, Roger slumped back into his commodious chair. More kindly designed than Vanessa's perch, which it was supposed to match, it shielded him. He started a summary of his meeting with the humble entomologist with whom he had lunched and who, having ordered a vast meal, had even contrived to attach a packet of cigarettes on to the bill. Then he opened his desk's top drawer and fingered the fragment of newspaper on which the vacancy was described.

Roger wanted to get away before his mind became completely blunted by New Vision's formulae and before Maureen's sloganeering drove him spare. A job at this more gentlemanly publishing house, where books still had footnotes despite the cost and there might be others sensitive to fine French wine, would suit him better. It would be a step in the right direction.

Like Maureen, Roger had his daydreams, but because they did not entail time travel, they were marginally more realistic. He liked to imagine himself as a writer of screenplays residing in the south of France. From his comfortable retreat he would assault the modern syllabus of errors and his pronunciamentos on 'women's lib' would receive the respectful attention of the world. The excellent good taste of his everyday life would be featured regularly in the Sunday colour supplements:

> I get up very early in the morning — usually around five — because at that time I can truly imagine that I am the only person alive in the world. I take Akbar, my Labrador whose grandmother belonged to Ian Fleming, for a long walk through a good truffle forest before breakfast. For that I have a warm croissant with strong French coffee and while I am eating I sometimes read the foreign reviews that my publisher sends me, but only if I'm in the mood. Ernestine, my Proustian helpmeet, does not disturb me until. . . .

The sorry fact that his wife did not naturally figure in his fantasies worried Roger slightly. And while he was trying to accommodate her in this one Vanessa interrupted him. She cupped her phone and told him there was an irate indexer on the line who had not been paid.

'Tell her the invoice is stuck in accounts,' he said. Then he rummaged in his in-tray, which he had not been able to face for a couple of days. His ashtray began to overflow as he began the painful research necessary for a serious job application. Could he still say fluent French, or was it now well and truly a mere 'working knowledge'? As Laura hovered about him in search of a German dictionary, he hastily scribbled over his calculations.

'You look worried, Roger,' she said.

He gave her his vulnerable smile and started again.

Vanessa shoved a load of letters at him and he signed them all. Then, co-operatively, he went to the coffee table to dump his dirty mug. On his way back he complimented Vanessa on her blouse. Dutifully, she smiled.

Five-thirty came and, as usual, Maureen was the first to clatter out with her collection of carrier bags. Vanessa disappeared into the lavatory and Roger fished in her bin to retrieve her *Daily Mail*. At six o'clock the room was deserted and he approached the electric typewriter. Straddling the tiny seat he aimed a finger and typed his date of birth.

CHAPTER THREE

Maureen reckoned that luck had brought Fabian Kemp into her life, but a sociologist, or Fabian for that matter, might have considered that their meeting was only a question of inevitability. The setting for their first encounter certainly suggested this.

As a conscientious newcomer to London, Maureen had set and applied herself to the task of sampling the old imperial capital's glut of intellectual plant: the galleries and the museums, the historic buildings and the cinemas. One wet Saturday morning found her in a small cinema that had advertised a day's worth of Werner Herzog films for the price of one.

In the middle, chronologically at least, of *Fata Morgana*, the image on the screen melted before her and the lights came on. A muffled voice from the projectionist's box announced technical difficulties and two options for the small audience: getting their money back or arranging to come to another screening of the same films on the following weekend. Maureen had moaned too audibly and she felt too lethargic to leave the warm building promptly. She peered at the reviews in the foyer noticeboard and tried to summon up an alternative inclination for the day. Fabian stood beside her and she remembered thinking that he looked like a student in his shabby duffle coat. He asked her if she knew of a place nearby where he could get a 'good cup of coffee'. She was of no help to him, but they walked to the nearest Underground together and found themselves agreeing to meet at the re-screening.

In Maureen's company Fabian felt relaxed and unusually confident. After several more trips to the cinema with her, he had offered her a room in the flat that his mother had bought him in Kentish Town. This offer had been made in a chivalrous and genuinely platonic spirit, because for some reason, which was never articulated, there was no sexual dimension to their friendship.

Like Maureen, Fabian was restless, but in his case this stemmed, not from an anxiety about finding a niche, but from an indecisiveness about whether to justify or evade the one that he had been born into. Unlike Maureen, Fabian was not trying to escape from a black pepperless world of processed foods, laminated surfaces and mispronunciation, and he cheered her with his instinctive adherence to certain standards and his easy disregard for others. He insisted on real coffee despite an income based on part-time teaching and only intermittently realized aspirations as a photographer. He did not worry about bad breath, no matter how much garlic he had eaten, and he left new hardback books for perusal in the toilet.

Reluctant to fall in with her ethnic identity because of her vague but nagging ambitions as well as her treacherous loss of the Faith, Maureen needed to find allies within the host culture and Fabian provided England with one of its most congenial faces. This was important, given her paranoia about aspects of British life. When the local pub had displayed Union Jacks on the occasion of some royal anniversary, for example, Maureen had backed off because she assumed that it had become an enclave of the racist lumpenproletariat. Sometimes also she had bad dreams in which, like medieval townspeople turning against a heretical scapegoat, loyal subjects tore her from limb to limb. But Fabian, as a representative of a liberal (albeit minority) component of the culture, alleviated these phobias.

For his part, Fabian found Maureen's petit-bourgeois lapses endearing. On the whole, she was easy to live with and there was something almost primevally comforting about her command of their steamy kitchen with a Sunday joint belching in its oven. He was more amused than offended by the blatancy of Maureen's occasional efforts to capitalize on his connections.

Fabian's mother, Dolores, was the second wife of a well-known novelist by the name of Clive Riley. Her first husband and the father of her son was Gus Kemp, professsor of linguistics at an Australian university. Before emigrating there he had been one of England's first self-made academics, the species that put working-class life on the country's cultural map as a valid new 'tradition'. Dolores would recall that Gus had had distinctly social-democratic tendencies, hence Fabian's name, and she suspected that her son had inherited his father's cunctatious spirit. But when Dolores accused him of being soft, Fabian retorted by saying that it had been easier for Dolores's generation to be rigorous. In an inflation of meanings, he said, it is less easy to be sure.

Formally, Dolores Riley insisted that her children be independent, but she resented it when they took this injunction too seriously. Dolores had reared Cassiope – Clive's daughter by his first marriage – so she regarded her as a child of her own. Cassiope's natural mother was a Paris-based polemicist who had devoted much of her recent life to the exposure of what she called 'the cultural determinants of the so-called maternal instinct'. It amused Dolores to suggest that by breeding so true at such a distance, Cassiope had somehow undermined her natural mother's project. If there was no such thing as innate proclivities, such as the maternal instinct, how had Cassiope come to behave just like the first Mrs Riley?

Fabian had disappointed his mother by not getting very

involved with Oxford student life. But although he found it difficult to make close friends, nobody disliked him, and he had the insurance of many well-wishers among the young people who would form the future mediating cartels of London. When he had come down, Dolores found him a job with a design magazine and he had stuck it out for eighteen months in order to convince her that his one consistent ambition had been born of some experience in the real world.

There was a thin spring light shining as Maureen walked home from the Underground on the evening after her lunch with Martin, and the winter's waning was marked by the children who were still playing in the shabby street where she and Fabian lived. From its farthest end she could hear the *Greensleeves* jingle of the pink ice-cream van that was parked outside the house, which was divided into two flats.

When Maureen first tried to tell Fabian about her upbringing, it had seemed right to start by informing him that the residents' association of Beech Hill had successfully banned all ice-cream vendors from the area on account of the noise and their concern about their children's teeth. She remembered feeling sad about the banishment of the ice-cream men with their curiously sexual names: Mr Ripple, Mr Creamy, Mr Whippy and Mr Softee. In Beech Hill the footprints of individual local dogs, carelessly immortalized in wet cement, could be identified. Its residents were not assailed by endless circulars advertising 'Oxford' schools of typing and English, and nothing could be kept secret. It lay worlds apart from the London of bad plumbing and all-conquering cats that was Fabian's heartland.

Maureen had been the apple of her accountant father's eye. Her brother had been oppressed by her father's ambitions for him, but she exceeded his hopes simply because he had not thought of holding any for his daughter. She was never brilliant because she always stopped short of the gamble of profundity, but she was very efficient. Her father's aggressive individuality – he insisted on keeping the old wooden toilet seat long after all the neighbours had bright plastic ones with fluffy covers – sometimes embarrassed her, but in general she was proud of him.

In the Ryan home Maureen's father had had 'special category status'. The kitchen table, where he used to sit before his own special salt cellar and an unusually large knife and fork while conducting mealtime conversations like a service, had been a veritable altar to patriarchy. When she first encountered feminism Maureen had found it ironic that her deficiencies in all things mechanical and quantitative, which sprang in her case from the glory of a paternal tradition, were the stereotypical ones of women in general and, in England, of all Irish people. Maureen felt orientated towards men because she associated a certain wild and speculative mode of conversation, like her father's, with their company. But the highly domesticated and quietly intelligent Fabian, offered a novel brand of masculinity.

She found him in their kitchen mending a puncture on his bicycle.

'You never told me about this party,' she said accusingly. Fabian turned and looked at her blankly.

'I never told you about what party?'

'Clive is having a party this weekend. Laura Kershaw told me.' (She could not say that Martin had told her in case Fabian would read her interest in the party too clearly.)

'Oh Christ, you don't want to go to that, do you? Believe me, it will be full of miserable shits with enormous egos. You'd hate it.' Despite his vehement language, Fabian said this very calmly.

'Of course, I want to go,' she said, 'You know I'd like to

meet your folks. I've heard so many stories about them and it's silly knowing so much about people I've never met. Besides, there's nothing else happening on Saturday.'

'Poor alienated creature,' he said mockingly, 'you always have to have something happening. You're not happy unless it's lunchtime, or night-time, or the weekend. But he smiled at her as he said this and wiped his hands on the anti-racist slogan of his tee-shirt. Then she was confident that they would go because she knew he would be curious to see what she made of his mother's house.

While Maureen Ryan was wondering what to wear to the party a young man of her own age with very different preoccupations was walking through a deserted municipal park. The silence, broken only by the occasional half-hearted *whoop whoop* of an arthritic swan, was unusual and as he kicked a squashed milk carton in the direction of the nearest litter bin, Lionel Trent was questioning the value of the discipline he had imposed upon himself.

Because he was unemployed, Lionel thought it important to rise early each day and adhere to a regular schedule, but this was a Saturday morning. Normally the park at this hour would have been alive with proudly trim young mothers, pushing first-born babies in flimsy buggies. No sober male adults between the ages of thirty and fifty would have been seen because the park was a microcosm of the capital's demographic and economic trends.

For the past six months Lionel had been living in an intensely local world. He passed through the park on his way from the Edwardian swimming baths where, every morning at the same time, he did twenty-one lengths, seven each of the three strokes he could perform. It was his habit to buy a cup of tea from the kiosk near the park bandstand, but this was closed on Saturday mornings. Then he usually visited the nearby Gentlemen's lavatory, an impressive redbrick building, erected, he had been told, by a zealous local temperance committee in the days when it was thought that men, breadwinners, were tempted into public houses on account of their sanitary facilities.

From the historic Gentlemen's, Lionel usually made his way to the library to read the daily newspapers – like many of the unemployed, he was unhealthily well-informed. He was also aware of the days when specialist journals arrived in the library, usually a week after publication, and this Saturday morning he braced himself in expectation of a certain publishers' weekly, which could yet hold out the promise of a job for a young man with an average degree in social anthropology.

As usual, the library was empty of adults and the librarian on duty greeted Lionel in grateful recognition. Before him on a desk he set out three curriculum vitaes. The first, which he generally sent out in pursuit of the vacancies appearing in the socially aware publications, suggested that Lionel was an energetic (the swimming) and a caring (his voluntary work at the local old folks' home) sort of person, and it played down his rather superfluous education. The second curriculum vitae was more desperate. In it Lionel laid claim to the personality of a 'self-starting all-rounder' and his captaincy of a school debating team at the age of fifteen found a mention. The third document, which he held as he pondered the job of 'trainee proofreader' with Golden Sheaf Books, was more honest in so far as it was not seriously misleading, being only guilty of the sin of elision – the nervous breakdown that had forced him to interrupt his degree for a year was disguised as a language-learning sojourn abroad.

Although he had become too depressed to believe in the possibility of paid work and now focused his hopes on a course in Computer Studies he had applied for, Lionel decided to photocopy the publishing vacancy. He could leave it on the kitchen table where his mother would see it and perhaps reassure herself that he was trying hard. He

knew that back home on the same table she would have left
a scoured newspaper of her own, reflecting on the one
hand a touching pride in him – the heavily-ringed ad-
vertisement for a lecturer's job at Durham University –
and on the other a bitter contempt – the X-ed box
required 'boys' to help in a furniture warehouse.

Lionel could remember having read somewhere that
Napoleon's handwriting had cut through the manuscripts
that he wrote his orders on and his mother's script had this
menacing intensity. He knew that he troubled her. She had
given him the name Lionel (his more sentimental father
had wished to commemorate some Mayo uncle) in order to
give him an upward start in life. It was true that he had
made it to university, but he seemed too sloppy and cynical
to be a graduate. (Mrs Trent's notions about graduates
were derived from television dramas set in 1920s Ox-
bridge.) All that Lionel could offer was an extra politeness
to the few neighbours she was on speaking terms with, so
that at least she could enjoy some satisfaction in their
approval of him. He could feel his mother's reproachful
eyes boring into his back as he squeaked across the library
floor to the copying machine that hummed laboriously in
the corner.

Fingering the change in his pocket, he raised its rubber
cover. But there was something beneath it, a hardback
notebook that looked as if it had once suffered immersal in
water. He picked it up and read the address inscribed on its
endpaper: C. Riley, 22 Tolpuddle Square. The little book
seemed to function as an address book, though it was an
address book with a difference. Wonderingly, Lionel
perused the 'B' section: Beckett, Bretécher, Berger, Bertol-
ucci, these were recognizably the surnames of eminent
people, but there were others, possibly just as illustrious –
the Laura under K and the Chantalle under P – jostling
alongside them. All the entries were scrawled out in a
childish and occasionally illiterate handwriting.

Lionel was excited. He wanted to meet the compiler of this book, which was possibly the work-hunting dossier of a more enterprising person than himself. But there was no one else in the library. After looking around for a likely owner, he left the book on the copying machine and went back to his desk, glancing up every now and then to see if its owner had returned. He spent half an hour drafting an abject letter of application to Golden Sheaf Books before going to the fiction area in order to select his mother's reading matter for the coming week.

Mrs Trent liked historical fiction without unromantically explicit sex. Her taste ran to heaving bosoms, tremulous embraces and orgasmic kissing, but she shunned the portrayal of activities below the waist, or rather bodice. Lionel had to vet likely works before he could risk taking them home to her. She read the same novels again and again, but there had to be an interval of about three months between her repeated immersals in Renaissance passions. He picked up a Lucretia Borgia number and a biography of Anne Boleyn, neither of which she had seen since Christmas, before returning to the still ghostly reading room end of the library.

It was time to go home. The librarian was preparing to close up and giving her lone reader discreetly imploring looks. Lionel went over to the machine and picked up the address book. There was a plastic carrier bag leaning against the machine's base, which, a furtive investigation told him, contained a typed document, so he put the address book in it and took the whole lot away with him. Lionel was curious and he reckoned that he could easily replace these mysterious goods back where he had found them on Monday morning.

His mother was home ahead of him. She was the receptionist in a local driving school and in her lunch breaks she sometimes went in and out of shops in the high street, asking their proprietors if they had a 'start' for a smart lad with three 'A' levels. Muriel Trent had been a widow for sixteen years and it was her wish to retire in the near future to Jersey, where her sister ran a small knitting shop. But she would not go, she insisted, until Lionel was 'settled' and he felt that he would never get a job while she wanted him to so desperately.

They ate together quietly. He told her about the proofreading job, but not about the address book. She looked at him critically when he announced that it was his intention to read that afternoon. Books have done you no good up to now, she was thinking as she shrewishly removed the butter that he was spreading too liberally on his bread. She oscillated between condemnations of Lionel as an inadequate human being and condemnations of politicians, but when her assault was focused on him alone, Lionel usually backed away. As he stepped upstairs to his bedroom, he was thinking, not for the first time, what a pity it was that his mother was godless.

To marry her Irish shoe salesman Muriel Trent had found it necessary to graft a pragmatic Catholicism onto a thin Anglicanism, but the observances that were fitfully honoured in the haziest days of Lionel's childhood were abandoned after his father's death. His mother had never seriously lost her other faith, however, and she retained a trust in the political party she always voted for in the face of an ever-widening incongruity between her income and her social status as she perceived it. Against renewed adversity she mustered up a lonely and bitter spirit of self-sacrifice, while her newer neighbours enjoyed an exuberant solidarity in homespun revivalist chapels. The street now held few acceptable allies for Mrs Trent, just the nice old couple living across the street and goodhearted Mrs Creasy who, though tainted by the drinking trouble that set in after her husband left her to the mercies of her unruly children, was none the less white and of 'clean-handed' stock.

Mrs Trent did not understand the quotation from *Capital* overhanging Lionel's bed, which bleakly prophesied that 'the generalization of popular education makes it possible to recruit this line of labourers (clerks) from classes that had formerly no access to such education and that were accustomed to a lower standard of living,' and that 'at the same time this generalization of education increases the supply and thus competition.' She thought this text was some sort of exhortive motto and seeing Lionel so cheerfully examining the contents of the library carrier bag, which he had emptied out over his bed, another observer might have agreed with her assessment.

As he began to study the address book again, Lionel lit a cigarette. His mother − a chain smoker herself − did not approve of smoking in the upstairs rooms and he knew that there was a risk that she might soon peer round his bedroom door and sniff the air disapprovingly, just as she used to in the most onanistic days of his adolescence. After an hour or so, he felt tired, so he pulled the curtains and drifted off to sleep.

It was dark when Lionel woke up in sudden possession of the reason why the name inside the address book had seemed familiar. He turned on the light and reached for his bookshelf, pulling out a slim paperback novel with a picture of a voluptuous young girl sucking an ice-cream cone on its cover. It was one of Clive Riley's more recent works, telling the (somewhat autobiographical) story of a middle-aged man trying to cope with a nubile and wayward young daughter while on vacation in the south of France. Several summers previously, Lionel had bought it at a station bookstall and he had found parts of it mildly erotic. It had been published in 1976, but the blurb was not very informative. It simply declared that Clive Riley (alias C. Riley?) lived in London with his wife and their two children, and that he enjoyed making wine. Lionel looked up Tolpuddle Square in the *A-Z of London* and found it in

Camden Town. Then he heard his mother calling him down to dinner. He put out a cigarette and poured water into the ashtray, which filled the room with a foul smell.

Mrs Trent looked surprised when he rose decisively after their meal and announced that he was going to visit 'some friends' that evening. She knew his giro usually came on Tuesdays and she did not think he had any friends, not in London at any rate. She removed the old cotton gloves she had put on in readiness for the library books he had brought her — she said that they protected her from other people's germs — and reached for a red plastic purse. She gave him two pounds and the remains of her packet of cigarettes.

'Will you be out long?'

'No, I'll be on the last Tube at the latest.'

She nodded and watched him pick up the carrier bag. Then, uncharacteristically, he kissed her on the forehead. Although she found this gesture embarrassing, she kept up her smile until he had left.

CHAPTER FOUR

————————————— ✳ —————————————

When Dolores and Clive Riley first bought their home in Camden the area was not yet even up and coming: they were vanguard gentrifiers. They had knocked down walls within their tall, double-fronted house and lined those that remained with large framed posters. Exposed pipes had been painted in vivid colours and every visible piece of woodwork had been stripped of generations of magnolia gloss. Extra character had been lent to their interiors by items pillaged from the indifferent natives of several continents: a Mexican altar rail served as an upstairs bannister, Dolores chopped vegetables on the oak from a sixteenth-century French barn and Indian rugs adorned their studies. Number 22 Tolpuddle Square was now interestingly comfortable and not *too* clean. Though Dolores and Clive puzzled their elderly neighbours by moving naked around their lace-curtain-less bedroom, successive burglars had seen the good taste behind the endearingly shabby façade (and posed the dilemma of a liberal perspective on crimes against property).

On the evening of the Riley party Maureen was excited, just as she had been before the first 'mixed' parties of her adolescence. She spent nearly an hour mincing up and down in front of her encouragingly damaged mirror before sauntering into Fabian's room in a vivid scarlet flamenco skirt and a white broderie Anglaise blouse. But to her chagrin Fabian, who was not dressed any differently than usual, talked matter-of-factly about the possibility of salvaging leftover party food to take back with them. And though Maureen would have liked to have been transported to the party in a carriage (a taxi would have done), like some Tolstoyan heroine, instead she experienced the mundane intermission of a crowded bus ride.

Dolores opened the door. Clive (at least Maureen guessed that it was he) waved an arm at them from the kitchen, where he was talking on the telephone. Fabian's mother was large and robust. A great mass of thick iron-grey hair was piled luxuriously on top of her head and in her richly embroidered Afghan dress she brought to mind portraits of Renaissance personages, whose prestige was indicated by the textures and embellishments of their clothing rather than the slimness of their hips.

When she heard that Maureen was 'in publishing', Dolores proclaimed it *the most immense* shame (her parlance was punctuated with superlatives) that she would not have the chance, that evening, of meeting Cass who was doing research in New York. Dolores had Maureen pinioned against the hall wall until she had ascertained as best she could that there was no carnal connection between Maureen and her mysteriously chaste son. She was free to break away from Dolores's throaty authoritativeness and make a proper entrée only after more guests had arrived and begun to cram the narrow hallway.

In the centre of the very large room that led off from it, Clive Riley was dispensing punch. As he poured generous glassfuls, he gestured good-humouredly at his home-made wine and reassured his guests that he would not take offence if they declined to sample it in the course of the evening.

His skin, which shone with the permanent tan of middle age, seemed to hang in terraces on his cheeks and his mouth opened and shut rapidly around small and barely visible teeth. He was compellingly ugly, a *jolie laide* man, and his posture beside the drinks table reminded Maureen of the dancing master in a Degas painting – a man with spats and stick presiding over a hall full of beautiful young girls in midi-length tutus – which had adorned the lid of an old chocolate box used by her mother for storing reels of cotton. Maureen herself could affect high cheekbones by holding her mouth in a certain way, or so she thought when she practised in front of a mirror, and she wondered if Dolores's vehement lips or Clive's intelligent squint had once been the conscious affectations of youth.

Fabian, who for all his nonchalance felt queerly paternal in his attendance upon Maureen at this stage in the evening, urged her forward and introduced her to the dancing master.

A familiar 'bridging' personality of television culture and a favourite selector of newspaper new-year book lists, Clive Riley was an adroit fish in a very stagnant pond. He had comfortable reserves of fat still stored up from his creative hey-day nearly two decades earlier and as a generous encourager, promoter and critic of those coming after him, he had acquired a licence to canonize other literary aspiranti. Clive was what Stanley H. Ruckster salivated over, a 'household name'.

Clive's chief initial awareness of Maureen was unfortunately predictable. She was not, as he so indelicately (and inaccurately) put it, 'from this British isle'. Maureen shuddered inwardly, imagining the double-edged stereotype that had risen up in his head: a drunken and irrational violence on the one side, and a verbose romanticism on the other. It was rather like the woman/intuitive, man/logical antonym and she resented the implicit condescension.

Misinterpreting her unease, Clive immediately added that he himself was part Irish (she had guessed this anyhow from his surname). He told her that his distant (and therefore tolerable) Hibernian forebears had got into a good racket as corn stevedores on the expanding docks of mid-nineteenth-century London. He seemed to speak in inverted commas much of the time, which gave his utterances the quality of a jaded hedonism, and like Dolores he had an uncomfortably direct gaze. Less shrewd than his wife, however, Clive imagined that his stepson had got himself a fine thing in this, for his taste too thin, but none the less striking-looking girl.

Among the many social privileges deriving from his status as an intellectual magistrate was Clive's right to initiate a conversation on any topic of interest to him and to drop it if he became bored. He could assume that his audience was either interested or informed. This assumption was obviously justified in the case of Maureen who, he judged from her defensive stance, was certainly not innocent of him. Consequently, Clive ignored the guests who were now jostling around him like expectant pilgrims around a great curative shrine and he began to tell Maureen of his attempts many years earlier to learn Gaelic.

'Of course,' he said, 'I never got the *blas* quite right and the people teaching me were so exclusivist about it. I mean, I'm allowed to speak French even though I'll always sound like an Englishman. The Irish are positively Jewish about their language.'

As Maureen was forming a jerky gesture of sympathy, Dolores moved purposefully in on them. She would not allow Clive to squander his social capital on an obscure friend of Fabian's and she was pulling behind her two *grattissima* arrivals: Martin and Laura Kershaw. Pushed onto the periphery, Maureen was grateful for Laura's smile of recognition because it meant that her integration was more truly faked, but she refused to look directly at Martin. Instead she took in Laura's appearance.

Laura Kershaw evoked a chameleon-like response from the world. People lowered their voices when they spoke with her and listened attentively to what she had to say.

She had that indefinable natural elegance, which the English so generously ascribe to the French. Quite nondescript, even shabby, garments compromised for Laura and colours leaned towards her in a special effort to bring out the wise grey-blue of her eyes. On this evening her hair was, slightly ineptly, coiled in a low Virginia Woolf-style knot and she was wearing a soft, pink wool dress. In scuffed but sensuous black suede shoes, she seemed taller than usual.

Dolores approved of Martin and Laura, although she could not restrain in herself an occasional bitchiness about Laura's refusal (unlike her own) to be openly supportive of Martin's careerist manoeuvres. When she had found out that she had conceived Fabian, Dolores had had an uncomfortable premonition that her child would not be some improved by-product. This feeling was confirmed when Fabian turned out to be deplorably visual, a distruster of words. But Martin was more like the person Fabian ought to have become.

Maureen was now hovering uneasily about the room, a double failure because of her numbness with Clive and uncool effusiveness towards Laura. She surveyed the crowded scene and pondered on the elements of style. A kind schoolteacher had once advised her to counteract feelings of intimidation by imagining the offenders sitting on toilets. But this homely advice was redundant in a world where tampons were kept conspicuously in the lavatory and unlockable doors were de rigueur. She thought that she should have more to drink.

Conversations at Tolpuddle Square were always politely tinged with a certain political radicalism, but an unspoken rule of delicacy was being broken around the drinks table where the revolutionary deficiencies of the British working class were being loudly debated. A petulant man accused a woman, who was aggressively chewing French bread with pâté, of being like a parent on a visit to boring relatives, wanting the children (the working class) to kick up a row and demand to leave so as to be spared the necessity of taking a rude initiative herself.

Their artful intensity made Maureen suspect that this was an argument between two people who wanted to end up in bed together as soon as possible, so she did not try to join in. Instead she moved on again, passing through discussions about home births and the incidence of vermin among modern children, before finding herself back in Dolores's ambit.

Dolores was commanding Laura and Martin to visit the Riley retreat in Provence in the coming summer. Laura, toying with the jade bangle around her wrist with the distracted concentration of a mother disentangling a child's shoelace, was being non-committal.

'It's kind of you to ask us over again,' she said, 'but we can't decide until we know what Martin's trip to New York after Easter entails.' Dolores turned towards Martin, who was annoyed at Laura's cautious response to the Provence invitation but at the same time unsure about the advisability of expressing vigorous enthusiasm.

'Oh well,' Dolores boomed. 'You really must pop in on Cassiope when you are there. You know that she has Herbert's apartment while he is in Africa. She absolutely loves the place, says it's so alive.'

With that last word Dolores raised her cigarette in a sort of salute and, as if it were her cue, an auburn-haired woman who spoke with a foreign accent homed in on their trinity.

This was Helly Branstorm, 'menstrual artist' and mother of two prematurely polysyllabic children, the youngest of whom had yet to show signs of a capacity to overcome the effects of a video show focused around his potty training. Helly had first achieved notoriety during the public outcry over an institution called the Blood Shed. Sanguinary linen flags still announced this converted warehouse in London's

East End as a haven for dysmenorrheal women. There they could contemplate Helly's works, most infamously, the giant swollen tampon stretched across a ten-foot-high cross in parody of Christ crucified; sip Bloody Marys from the comfort of hammocks designed to look like oversized sanitary towels; or receive the 'wise wound' counsels of fully initiated Dianic witches.

After a year-long campaign, Helly's Blood Shed won out against accusations of blasphemy and obscenity, and she found herself welcome in the most exclusive salons of North London. Now she was careful to salute Martin Kershaw with respect, for they were equal in their status on this night as junior members of Clive's entourage.

Helly's proximity made Martin nervous, however, because he had once told her that he wrote fiction under an assumed name. It had been a mistake, done in the false solidarity of a drunken evening they had spent together, and now he was like the mythical king at the feast, waiting for the harp made from his confessional tree to sing to all the assembled of his shame. Whenever he found himself in Helly's company, Martin usually tried to move away.

The music, in the beginning at background volume, was now louder and some of the more miscellaneous of the Riley's guests – those with no specific 'business' to do – had been tempted to the polished dancing floor at the far end of the big room. Martin sought Maureen's eye and in desperation – Fabian was nowhere to be seen – she allowed him to catch it, walking a little stiltedly with him towards the dancers because of a fear that her blouse would pull out of the waistband of her skirt.

Laura, Helly and Dolores were joined by Clive. Helly started to tell them about the exhibition of her children's drawings of female sexual parts, which she was currently organizing.

'My philistine mother threw out all my juvenalia,' Clive wailed mockingly, 'and now I feel sure I could interest

Ralph Newman in the religious period I went through at
the age of fourteen.'

The women smiled, but before Helly could continue,
Dolores was introducing more guests to Clive. Laura gazed
over the conversation at Maureen and Martin's awkward
caper. From experience she knew that Martin was merely a
rhetorical flirt. So far, to her knowledge, no woman had
been bold or foolish enough to take him up on his
innuendos, but Maureen, she thought, might be different.
She was a sharp little thing, as capable of slipping into any
ready crevice as she could wriggle through the tightly-
spaced bars of a park fence.

Still uncomfortably aware of her blouse's unruly potential, Maureen felt sandwiched between Laura and Martin.
It was like her childhood experiences on dodgem cars, half-
thrilling and half-terrifying. When Clive scuttled by them
with Helly as his navigator, she was sure that she heard
Martin moan and, as if he sensed her observation, he seized
her fervently around her waist and began to kiss her neck.
Maureen was aghast. He was like the fabled ostrich,
burying his passionate head in her neck and imagining
himself unseen.

'Why are you so nervous tonight, darling little Maureen,' he muttered savagely into her ear. Martin's embarrassment about what Helly knew made him feel sadistic
towards Maureen, but then he felt ashamed of himself.

'Don't worry,' he said in a softer voice, 'everyone is
terribly sophisticated here.'

When he placed one of his hands on her left breast,
Maureen wanted to run away, but there was no sign of
Fabian. She gazed dumbly at him until she spied Laura,
laughing while her hair was being loosened by the
apologist for the British working class. Then she smiled up
at Martin and decided to trust him. He fetched her another
drink, and she gulped it down. They ignored the music and
lurched around the room according to an obscene tempo of

their own. Maureen imagined that she was becoming more beautiful under his eyes, that her skin was becoming whiter and smoother, and that her triangular eyes were brighter and pointier. As she became more oblivious to their surroundings, she began to reciprocate his caresses.

They were not left alone like this for long, however, and afterwards Maureen was to wonder if Clive and Helly's officious interruption had displeased Martin as much as it had her. Outraged elders reclaiming an abducted virgin, they had surged on top of them and then, pushing conversation up like phlegm, she was wheeled around the room by Clive in a bizarre 'follow the ashtrays' dance.

During one of Clive's abrupt halts she stole a backward glance to where she imagined Helly and Martin to be. She saw him nuzzling into Helly's neck and fondling her hair. Martin was busy exorcizing the last wince-provoking occasion with Helly by super-imposing another on top of it. Near them Maureen saw Laura, who was now teaching Helly's daughter how to jive. She kept a watch out for Fabian, all the time wary of Clive's warm breath in the way that she had been wary of a hideously affectionate old grandaunt. Eventually she bowed out of his grasp with a mutter about the loo and an inner thought that there was something positively portentous about the slight pain in her lower abdomen.

The lavatory-cum-bathroom was large. There was a huge marble washstand, which was garnished, like some propitiatory household altar, with an impressive array of expensive talcs and lotions, and a great font of a toilet. Maureen sat on its mahogany seat and began to sing:

> When we were savage, fierce and wild
> She came like a mother to her child
> But now we are all civilized
> Neat and clean and well-advised
> Oh won't Mother England be surprised!

As she searched in her memory for more words, she became aware of a man with green spectacle frames, who was grinning at her while he pissed into the coffin bath. She stayed put until he had gone. The toilet bowl was bright red and she gleefully crept back downstairs with the damp, tadpole tail of a tampon between her legs.

At that moment Lionel Trent was standing apprehensively in the porch with the address book in one of his hands and the plastic carrier bag in the other. Rudely parked cars and the sound of drunken voices had alerted him to a party in the vicinity as he was entering Tolpuddle Square, and he felt a sense of relief when he discovered that Number 22 was its site. Even so, he knocked on the door instead of using the bell in the irrational hope that he might draw less attention to himself that way.

Maureen threw the door wide open.

'Come in, come in,' she said, still singing in her head. 'It's all happening now.' Because of Martin's betrayal of her with Helly, she felt annoyed with herself for having played up to him, and Clive's home-made wine, which she had tasted out of politeness, was beginning to take effect. She made Lionel drape his wet anorak over the hall radiator and he put the address book on top of it. Then she found him a glass of tepid punch, which he accepted from her humbly. She had decided to adopt this sodden stranger as her champion (there was no sign of Fabian).

'Which one is Clive Riley,' Lionel asked.

'Over there,' Maureen gestured through the party room's open door at Clive with an air of languid familiarity. 'Aren't you part of the scene then?'

Something about the tone of her question made him say 'not really' instead of a straight 'no', and he followed her into the main salon meekly.

'What do you do?' was his next question.

'Oh, I'm a slave in a publishers,' was her careless reply. Then she said, 'I suppose you write,' and he smirked ambiguously.

Maureen abandoned Lionel soon in order to fetch him more to drink. From the drinks table she could see that Laura and Martin were standing close together, their bodies vertically aligned with the folds of the French window's heavy velvet curtains. She kept her eyes down and ladled out punch in a business-like manner. Then she returned to Lionel, who remained rooted to the spot where she had left him. Calculatingly, she assessed his potential as a diversionary presence. He was a little like Fabian, only more endomorphic, and he peered through his National Health frames in an endearingly short-sighted way. She was even prepared to find the faint smell of perspiration emanating from his wet clothes appealing.

After his third glass of punch – he had not had alcohol since the last time, three months' ago, he had seen the rump of his university friends in Brighton – Lionel began to feel unsteady. He asked Maureen to mind his cigarettes, or rather his cigarette, there was only one remaining of the packet his mother had donated, and she placed it intimately in the breast pocket of her blouse.

'How did you get here?' he asked.

She knew that he meant where did she come from and not what mode of transport had brought her to Tolpuddle Square, and she was considering how to duck an account of her arrival in London when he spoke again.

'My dad came from Mayo. I can remember him telling me that the Duke of Wellington, the Waterloo star, once repudiated his Irish birth by saying that if you are born in a stable you are not necessarily a horse.'

'No,' said Maureen. 'You could be a rat.' At this their conversation closed for a time, and so they moved towards the dancers. As she tried to respond to a reggae track he said, 'Well, you sure as hell ain't got natural rhythm,' in a country-and-western-style accent. She was surprised and she laughed and took his hand. The room was very crowded and she suggested that they took some air together. The room had become oppressively hot, but a desire to get away from Martin had motivated this proposal, which Lionel readily agreed to.

When Maureen had left him in order to fetch his third drink, Lionel had tried to approach Clive, but he had been deflated by the piercing scrutiny of the tall and fat woman, Mrs Riley he guessed, who was monitoring all introductions. He was happy to go along with Maureen's suggestion because he had lost confidence in his mission and hoped to salvage some enjoyment from the evening under her guidance. Accordingly, they waded, hand-in-hand, through the other dancers until Maureen successfully located the French windows and admitted them into the dark outside. They walked down slithery wrought iron steps and found themselves in a wet garden that smelled overpoweringly of cats.

Above them the party was visible like a giant television screen. Clive was safely in Dolores's custody and Martin was dancing smoochily with Helly again.

'It all looks very jolly from here,' said Lionel, 'like the parties they show in television commercials. We should rush in clutching a six-pack of lager in order to complete the scene.'

Then he fell silent again. He was very drunk now and becoming a little fretful about the enormous gaps in his thought processes. But she did not seem to mind. When he noticed that his glasses were wet, Maureen supplied him with a tissue and he was touched by the fact that she pulled it out of the same breast pocket in which she had so reverently placed his cigarette. While he was holding his glasses, he told her that he could not see very much without them and then she kissed him on his mouth.

Lionel put his glasses back on and retaliated. They

continued to kiss each other inquisitively until Maureen became aware of his erection and moved apart again. Not knowing him, she could not be sure how drunk he was. He looked upset, though, so she took his hand and they fell back onto the wet staircase.

'What do you write?' she asked.

Lionel wanted to tell her about his masterly letter of application to Golden Sheaf Books, but something stopped him. Perhaps it was her brittle cleverness and casual cynicism about the job that she had.

'I've come to show a novel to Clive Riley,' he said, after what seemed like another intolerably long pause.

'Is he encouraging?' she asked.

'I'll have to see. The thing is that I don't actually know him, just of him. As a matter of fact, nobody knows what I've written except you.'

Then he hiccuped violently and for one fearful moment Maureen thought that he might even be sick. But he was simply looking for his cigarette. When Maureen produced it he gave her a positively beatific smile of gratitude. As she was refusing his offer of a drag on the unfortunately sodden cigarette, the door behind them opened and Helly peered down.

'So that's where you've been you anti-social people,' she crooned, 'this is a party, remember?'

Although the whole party had scarcely been paralysed for the previous half-hour on account of the absence of these two marginal personalities, they solemnly walked back in, like a pair of animals entering Noah's Ark. Maureen immediately went to the bookshelf where she had left her drink, but Lionel could not remember what he had done with his. He looked at the pathetically small lady's watch, his mother's, on his wrist and said that he should go. He asked Maureen if he could phone her up 'some-time'. She gave him her work number and then took his, just to neutralize the suggestion. She was not sure whether she ever wanted to meet him again. But she stood with him in the hall while he collected his belongings. He took up the carrier bag and thrust it into her arms.

'See what you think of that,' he slurred.

Now Maureen became a little agitated. She rarely read fiction and this was a responsibility that she would not have taken on willingly. He did not seem capable of understanding her reluctance, however, so she took it from him, merely enquiring cautiously if he had another copy.

'Nope,' he said, and then he opened the door. The long strings of his anorak flagellated the hall wall as he called back to her: 'Live dangerously!'

Maureen decided to be more persistent in her search for Fabian. She found him in the kitchen drinking tea.

'Where have you been?' she demanded.

He told her that he had been perusing old photographs in his oedipal bedroom. There was a great pile of these on the table.

'Then I retired to the kitchen because certain individuals, who shall remain nameless, required privacy and resented my occupancy of a room with a bed in it and a lockable door.'

There was no devilment in Fabian's voice and Maureen was trying to extract the identity of the couple from him when Martin came into the kitchen. He glanced sheepishly at the pot of tea and Maureen poured him a cup. He ruffled her hair and asked Fabian if he agreed with him that Maureen was beautiful. But Fabian said nothing, and Maureen was thinking that Martin looked tired and almost cloyingly boyish.

Many kisses were exchanged before Fabian and Maureen eventually left Tolpuddle Square. Men that she did not know, and even Dolores, kissed her and Maureen wondered at the Judas-like etiquette of the inner circles.

Lionel practically skipped out of Tolpuddle Square. He

even hummed to himself, although his head had hammers in it and he was hoarse from talking over a crowded room.

'Fuck their discreet charm,' he yelled at a passing hedge. 'She's okay. I like her mouth.' Then, noticing that he had caught the attention of an elderly man who, with dubious moral hauteur, was gazing at him suspiciously while his dog crapped on the pavement, he became quiet.

All seemed to be going his way. He had not missed the last south-bound train, and as he grinned happily to himself on the platform a comradely soul offered him a cigarette. He did begin to feel a little rueful about the lies he had told Maureen concerning the novel, however, but he persuaded himself that it had been for the best. She had seemed impressed and he was sure that she liked him and that he could sort it out when he met her again. Lionel felt about his gamble rather like the normally careful woman who has risked pregnancy for some spontaneous jouissance, a little fluttering and at first easily dismissed anxiety.

The train deposited him in the midst of a close network of Pooterish Victorian streets, all named after the American Great Lakes, and soon he was within moments of his mother's house. As he stepped on to a pedestrian crossing Lionel was aware of a car that was approaching from what seemed like a reasonable distance, but that was the last thought in his head.

When the telephone rang just after midnight, Muriel Trent was dozing on the sitting room couch. Normally, she would have been asleep, or at least in bed, at that hour, but she had stayed up in the hope that Lionel would come back with the goodnight cigarette she craved. She forced open her eyes and stumbled towards the phone only to find herself unable to register sensibly with the speaker. Having ascertained that she, Muriel Trent, the mother and sole next of kin of Lionel Trent, was alone in her house, he rang off. She had barely rubbed the pins and needles out of her calves when the doorbell rang.

Two policemen, one big one and one little one, walked in. The big one marched purposefully towards the sideboard bottle of brandy that she kept for the occasional toothache, while the other gave her a cigarette. They were well versed in the solemn innuendoes of 'fatals' duty, and used to women like Muriel who could not take things in at first. She pulled her wrinkled skirt as far over her knees as she could and fretfully patted her dishevelled hair. She was excessively polite and even as they reiterated the fact of Lionel's death, she found herself composing a grateful citizen's letter full of their praises for the local newspaper.

The big one stayed behind in the house. He took her brandy glass from her and said that he would wake Mrs Creasy and get her to come over. The other one drove her to the hospital where Lionel had been brought. Luckily, he was the smoker. When she saw Lionel's body she was surprised. His face had not been damaged, indeed she could quite confidently have said that he looked happier than she had ever seen him.

Muriel was reluctant to accept the fact of her only son's death, smitten as she was by a horrible feeling, not of simple grief – she had known that once – so much as a sense of having been cheated. He had gone away before she had had a chance to explain herself.

Something about the expression on his face made her suspect that maybe there was an afterlife. As a reproachful spirit Lionel might be reading her innermost thoughts, finding out that she had not been entirely displeased by his death, that, in fact, she had often wished it. She felt indignant and sure that she was entitled to give her side of things, especially now that he could afford to be impartial.

In the first few weeks afterwards she was continually drawn to Lionel's room. She would sit on the edge of his bed and address the chair over which the blue jeans he had changed out of that Saturday evening were still draped. While she spoke, she plaited the fringes at the side of his bedspread.

'I mean I did everything I could for you, didn't I? I started work at sixteen, like most people. I didn't expect my mother to feed and clothe me until I was twenty-four years old. And, as you well know, it's not as if your Dad left me with much. When he died on me, I had to drive his memory from my mind in order to carry on. Of course, I know it wasn't your fault that you looked, even walked and spoke, like him. In fact Sylv always said you looked more like me, but I could only see him in you. That's why I kept sending you away to stay with her.'

Over and over again, she exhausted herself with speeches like this. One night she fell asleep in the little room, having persuaded herself that he had taken everything in. The next morning she surprised them at the driving school by arriving for work and during her lunch break she visited an estate agent's office.

CHAPTER FIVE

———————— ✳ ————————

On the morning after the party Maureen woke up feeling cheerful. She had no hang-over and she was buoyed up by the exuberance of her menstrual tide. She pushed the encounter with Lionel into a dim recess of her mind and smiled to herself as she dwelled instead upon Martin's final attentions. While she was engaging Fabian in chatty recollections of the evening she sat on the kitchen heater so as to simultaneously avail herself of its warmth and his responses. She wanted him to confirm all that she chose to remember of the occasion, but for some reason (possibly loyalty to Laura) he was resisting this demand.

Yes, at no stage had Maureen seemed unduly drunk to Fabian and, yes, he agreed that Martin had been in a 'funny' (this was unsatisfactorily unspecified) mood. As Fabian adroitly skirted around her Martin-focused nostalgia, it was more and more obvious to Maureen that he was refusing to condone her infatuation. He kept directing the conversation towards what seemed to him a more acceptable theme – Maureen's dramatic flirtation with the mysterious 'gate crasher'.

It transpired that Lionel was not known to anyone at Tolpuddle Square and that Clive and Dolores had noticed his presence with some amusement, at first connecting him with Fabian, then Maureen and finally the absent Cassiope. Maureen did not wish to talk about Lionel and the plastic bag he had presented her with was a huddled mass,

53

shrouded by an old acrylic shawl that smelled of cigarettes, in a corner of her room. She therefore adopted a more circuitous strategy.

'Laura looked well, didn't she? She seemed to know a lot of the people there.'

Fabian looked irritated. 'Why?' he said, 'I really mean why, are you so obsessed with the way people, especially men, react to you? You're only interested in Laura because she so palpably interests men. You live as if you were in a cage being watched all the time. Has it ever struck you that some people just get along with living, without stopping all the time to see if other people are watching them?'

He gathered up the Sunday papers and walked out of the room. Maureen sat in the kitchen for a while longer and thought about his exit with hurt contempt. Fabian was not blessed (or cursed) with either nostalgia or hope: he lived resolutely and sometimes tediously in the present. She decided to ignore him for the rest of the day. Later they would come together over lunch and pretend that there had been no rift.

As days passed, however, Fabian's remarks came back to Maureen and the small gloating triumphs of the party began to seem more ambiguous. Her optimism ebbed away like water from a bath tub as she winced at the memory of her attempts to be clever and regretted her passionate responses to Martin's overtures. He had not vindicated her with a phone call.

A sense of atonement drove her nearer Laura at work and as a result of this proximity she learned of Laura's short-sightedness. This discovery facilitated a new friendship by giving the cold shoulders, blank stares and irregular salutations that Maureen had sometimes met with from a lens-less Laura in the past an innocuous significance.

Under Laura's mantle Maureen felt shielded from

Roger's poisoned darts and safe from Stanley, who might otherwise have been tempted to crush her as an embarrassing reminder of his own beginnings. She envied Laura her immunity, her wry tolerance of male worship from a distance and she felt that she could learn something from her. Maureen was often tempted to ask her questions about Martin, but she refrained, not simply because Laura was married to her cheater, but because she suspected that Laura would find her questions meaningless.

Why, for example, had Martin told her so intensely — three times, no less, like St Peter's denial of his Lord — that he loved her when they were dancing? It would have been enough for him to have expressed a precise desire to see her again.

Mournfully, Maureen likened herself to a Jane Austen heroine, sitting with miserable stoicism in the rectory morning room while waiting for some narcissistic fop to remember her virtues. She bit her lip frequently and her spectacles remained perched on her nose long enough to cut a red V into its sides. She started to smoke, amateurishly pulling on cigarettes whose nicotine she did not yet appreciate. At lunchtime she wandered disconsolately through the streets of Covent Garden, like the soldier-forsaken girls of ballads, and her tearful eyes caught those of passing predatory men.

She felt exposed and vulnerable. When she attempted to cross busy streets, stationary lorries were revved up by their insouciant young drivers in order to startle her into a humiliating retreat. In impotent rage she decided that she hated all men and Martin in particular. She pondered in detail the desirability of some sort of purdah provision for them. Meanwhile, the question of payment for her work on the *Aspidistra* index remained and she was tormented by the likelihood that Laura would be delegated as the bearer of her cheque. To keep rein on these morbid preoccupations, Maureen tried to be busy socially. She even arranged to have lunch with Vanessa, who normally kept a distance from the 'creative' staff.

They found seats in a wooden-floored vegetarian restaurant and ordered salads. Jaunty in a red painter's beret and a green velour tracksuit, Vanessa was none the less uncomfortable as a target for randomly directed emotions and she thought that Maureen was definitely uptight about something, or some man. She poked savagely at the oily pulses mounded up on their plates and spoke too loudly. She spilled her apple juice and combed it around the table with a plastic knife before seizing Vanessa's napkin in order to stop it from cascading into both of their laps. Obtrusively, she stole sugar cubes and all the while she was bombarding Vanessa with questions without giving her a chance to answer any of them.

Vanessa wondered whether to tell Maureen about the progress of her current liaison — Maureen had told her obliquely about Martin — but she thought better of it. There was no point in pretending that this was a balanced meeting. Instead she asked Maureen sensitively if she had seen her 'friend' lately.

Maureen was comforted by Vanessa's enquiry because it suggested that her melancholia had some basis in a real relationship. At the same time, she was a little sorry that she had ever told Vanessa about the whole business because now it was impossible to reclaim it.

'Well,' she said, 'he's sort of receded for the moment. I think he's depressed actually and, of course, when he's like that he doesn't want to see anyone.'

Vanessa eyed her shrewdly. It was peculiar she thought, the way Maureen was enslaved by this crush, even though she was supposed to be liberated. She thought that it was quite obvious that she had nothing substantial going with this writer creep. Vanessa herself was more sensible with men, moving effortlessly from unemployed actors to senior civil servants and worrying more about her libido than her image so that the latter gained from this sense of priorities. She delicately touched her lips with a napkin, a fresh one that she took from another table, and nodded.

'That's a pity,' she said. 'But I don't know why you put up with these neurotic intellectual types.' Then she realized that she had made a mistake, for, of course, Maureen probably thought of herself as an intellectual.

Maureen sensed that Vanessa's sympathy was tinged with impatience, so she told her that she was fed up with Martin (not by name) anyhow and feeling generally bored with men. Boredom was something Vanessa understood very well and so they enjoyed the rest of their lunch break speculating about Roger's chance of another job.

Martin Kershaw rarely worked normal office hours and he was only vaguely aware of weekdays as individual segments of time because his own productivity was measured by an intermittent and highly selective sociability. He might as well have been a sun-determined, though cerebral medieval peasant, waking, working and sleeping according to a pre-industrial rhythm. His indifference to the working hours of ordinary people was partly responsible for the cruel lapses in his communications with people generally and Maureen in particular, but there was another reason.

Laura had of late been intimating thoughts of motherhood to him, a vocation that to his relief he had never previously suspected in her. She gazed wistfully at the infants of friends and talked with considerable animation about the merits of different forenames. She did not provoke him with a direct negotiation but kept up a barrage of suggestive reasoning. She donated a pint of her blood and suggested that he do likewise, telling him that it would be interesting to know his blood group. She had become more persistently ratty about his smoking and he suspected that she had taken up swimming in order to be fit for some anticipated ordeal. If he did not know well that it was her way to build him up slowly to a decision-making point, he would have been sure that she was already pregnant, despite the yellowing cap on their bedside table. He was trying to mobilize biases against her hankering.

Martin wanted to try New York where *Aspidistra* still had a respectable circulation. The truth was that the journal's hour was now passing. Already many of its supporters were going over (or at least two-timing) to another journal, *Modes and Moments*, which seemed destined to become as influential for the next decade as *Aspidistra* had been for the last two. Clive Riley, for example, was contributing to *Modes and Moments* and affecting what was in Martin's opinion a premature nostalgia for *Aspidistra*. He was realizing that what men like Clive offered as friendship was really a form of speculative investment, and the hope of some furtherance in New York was acting as a shock absorber against many recent jolts to his ego.

Martin was resolutely home-grown. English was the only language he spoke fluently and he was not *au courant* with the affairs of Eastern European dissidents and French feminists. The *Modes and Moments* set rejected what they alleged to be the political and theoretical deficiencies of British culture for the obscurantist (Marxist) subtleties of foreign ones. Martin affected scorn for this strategy and compared them with those high-born Victorian converts to Catholicism who had renounced their empiricist birthright in favour of exotic and equally ill-adapted Popist practices.

Despite these brave opinions and a not unfounded trust that the tide would soon turn in his favour again, Martin was nervous. By becoming associated with *Aspidistra* in his early twenties he had been a precocious success, but now he was conscious of being the last heir of a faltering dynasty. It was important to get to New York while his contacts were still sound and before Laura moved in for the kill – or rather conception. Accordingly, he was responding to her astrological charts and edgy musings with books about the Museum of Modern Art and accounts of women whose lives had been scarred by motherhood.

Laura wished to stay in London and at New Vision, where Stanley would do everything to make it easy for her to be the mother of a young child and a careerwoman. She was relatively happy there and came home each day with gossipy anecdotes instead of the deep sighs Martin remembered from her previous work. Indeed, his alienation from Laura's new confidence had facilitated his interest in other women, though with Maureen he could not tell if she was naturally playful or really after him. It had been a harmless divertissement, he reckoned, though one that ought to be stopped now because, since Laura's instincts had come out, it seemed plausible that every woman had them. In recent weeks Martin had developed a phobia about being near women, lest he impregnate them, but they appeared to suck him towards them.

This afternoon Martin was ensconced in the British Museum. He was researching his introduction to a book about Victorian literary homosexuals, but none of the books he had ordered had yet arrived. Distractedly, he gazed at the protein-fleshed, thick-haired American bluestockings who clustered around the catalogues and when one of them caught his eye, he rose from his desk and decided to go out for a coffee. The old porter on duty for the baggage check of the intelligentsia waved him through the security gate with the familiar deference of a gate-lodge keeper.

As he passed the phone booths Martin decided to ring Maureen. He was surprised to find himself agreeing to meet her on the coming Sunday afternoon – a meeting was not necessary or desirable – but he put his amenability down to the general air of winding-up finality that his affairs had taken since the New York resolution had hardened.

On Sunday Fabian thought that Maureen was at Camden Lock Market helping the friend who had escaped from publishing into the management of a secondhand clothes stall. Laura thought, though she had not been told directly because Martin told no straight lies, that her spouse was at the feet of Walter Hardy, an ageing *Aspidistra* luminary. But in reality Martin and Maureen were on a bus that was crawling through Archway.

Maureen had selected Highgate Cemetery as their destination, partly because of her awareness of Martin's interest in all things Victorian and partly because it seemed an appropriate setting for what she suspected would be a closing scene.

As the bus agonized past a gaunt Archway pub, Maureen pointed it out as a landmark in her family history, a place where migrant Ryans had met and drunk the fruits of their labours in the days of the Empire. Martin nodded. He had become fretfully aware that he had left his address book at home, so that Laura could ring him at Walter's if he were unaccountably late. Maureen fell quiet when she noticed his restlessness. She listened to the rabbi in a sable-trimmed hat who was doing his best with two small and fervently interrogative sons and then she studied the other passengers. When she was with Martin she had a heightened sensitivity to the nuances of life. Acutely observant, like the Victorian chroniclers whose 'low-life' vignettes Martin was so fascinated by, she wanted to jerk his attention to this and that face, and the passing buildings.

It was wet but not raining, one of those days when it must have been pouring early in the morning. The hilly lane that led down to the cemetery smelled damp and green. Their fingers were interlocked, but their hands felt incompatible, as if the gesture had been made just to fill up the gulf that lay between them. Martin had rung Maureen, in order, he said, to thank her and arrange for the payment of her indexing work. But she had negotiated a different kind of meeting. So even though it was not difficult now to imagine herself as the awkwardly sympathetic escort of a recently bereaved person, she clutched Martin's cold hand tightly because the clasp confirmed that this was a loaded assignation. Maureen had a mean and curiously gratifying sense of herself as they walked through the cemetery gates.

All around them the Johannas, Susannahs, Sarahs and Elizas commemorated on mildewed slabs were disappearing into woody undergrowth, their demise marked by the coy phrases – 'gone home', 'gone asleep', 'at rest' – of a more chaste age. One particularly confident epitaph made Maureen exclaim: 'They were so sure, her family, that she *was* a pure, wise, honest and lovely virgin!'

Martin laughed at her fervour and then they began to compose epitaphs for themselves, summaries of their lives and aspirations that sounded like entries in a lonely hearts column. Even so, the jollity was strained because Maureen found it hard not to be awed by the sleeping place, which brought back memories of childhood trips to her grand-father's grave when she had been rebuked for impiously jumping on other tombs. Now she restrained Martin from doing so, but he misinterpreted her anxiety. He put his arm around her and kissed her mouth.

Maureen was disappointed. His mouth felt hard and perfunctory and the kiss tainted her memory of the party when his tongue had seemed to melt eucharistically in her mouth. She was irritated by his sexual manners, his noblesse oblige, so she became more serious and silent, luring him farther inwards.

They crunched through old autumn litter, left dry because of the woody canopy overhead, with childish satisfaction. Then a meditative and very muscular male angel, who was presiding over the pigeon-shit stuccoed mausoleum of a dipsomaniacal horse-slaughterer, arrested them. Martin began to talk of heaven, the place where all the souls fled from bodies deposited here, were presumed to have gone.

'The Christian idea of heaven has never attracted me. It's too passive, a state of permanent sedation. No sex even, not like the Islamic paradise, where I could expect to be ministered to by countless nubile handmaidens.'

He said this with a wicked grin on his face and Maureen was irritated again. All talk and no action, she was thinking. Nevertheless, she continued on the same theme. She told him that, for her, heaven was a kind of pre-industrial utopia, like Pre-Raphaelite visions of socialism, a place devoid of electrical appliances and sewage systems.

'But it's certainly not boring,' she said. 'You'll have your own patch on earth to look after. You could choose somebody interesting to be a guardian angel for, like a sort of celestial probation officer.'

Then they imagined who they would like to watch over. Maureen said that she would prompt Stanley Ruckster to give enormous pay rises, but Martin was less forthcoming about the individuals he would have liked to have been in a position to nudge. Maureen was pleased: it was so much easier to talk now that she was being released from his spell.

She asked him about New York and he told her that it was to be a reconnoitring trip. When she enquired about Laura's feelings, he went moody. Sometimes it was as if he wanted to be thought of as an unattached man, but Maureen refused to comply with this delusion because to treat Martin like a free agent was in some way a denial also of her relationship with him. Laura had to have recognition before she could find any place, even a retrospective one, in his life.

'Now, mind you don't catch herpes over there,' was her

last remark, typically charged with the chirpy sophistication she thought he expected of her. Herpes was an affliction she had read about in one of Vanessa's magazines, but, as she left him standing at the bottom of Swain's Lane, Martin looked confused. It was obvious that he had found this remark a bit unsettling. When she tried to summon Martin's image up, he often wore this kind of expression, but Maureen was never sure whether he was genuinely puzzled, or whether he just looked that way when he was annoyed.

Weary, but gloriously unvanquished, even by the fact that Martin had decided to go home early, Maureen settled back into the bus home feeling like Jacob must have done after his wrestle with the angel. Now that Martin was gone, and his removal was soon to be confirmed geographically, she was lighter, though with the impaired mobility of a soldier who has been delivered of a gangrenous limb after a painful operation. She could return to her normal fantasies unbothered by the distraction of one that had haunted her because it had seemed technically realizable. She thought of Fabian with renewed esteem and affection, and resolved to write a letter to her parents.

When she got home, Fabian was not in, so she settled down to this task. Since she had not written home for some time, it was hard to remember the white lies she had to remain consistent with. For example, she had to cover herself against any spontaneous visitors by mentioning Fabian's existence, though only as the teacher brother of one of her flatmates. But having told how helpful he was about the flat, she realized that between the lines of her spare little letter her optimistic mother might find grounds for imagining that she was 'doing a line' with a teacher in London. She chuckled to herself as she licked its envelope.

She was still in a good mood when she went out to post

it and before returning to the flat she stepped into a phone box. An overpowering smell of male urine rose up around her as she fumbled in her bag for the piece of card on which she had written Lionel's telephone number. He had not phoned her as he had said he would, but she was feeling generous. Perhaps he was too shy to ring her?

A harassed-sounding woman said hello and she asked for Lionel.

'Are you a friend of his?' said the voice.

'Well, I only met him once actually. I mean I don't know him awfully well.' Maureen wondered why she should have bothered to explain herself to this woman and regretted the superfluous 'actually' and 'awfully'.

Then the voice spoke again.

'I'm afraid I've very sad news for you my dear, because Lionel was knocked down and killed by a car about three weeks ago. Mrs Trent is with her sister until next week. You're lucky to get through here, you know, because she prefers to leave the phone off the hook these days – afraid of more bad news I expect. I live in the same street, you see, just popped in to feed the cats and I put it on again in case one of my kids needs me.'

Lionel's death was announced in much the same way as a busy shop assistant informs a customer that a certain commodity has been sold out. Maureen supposed that it was very well-rehearsed news in Lionel's territory by now and she was unsure about what she should do. She needed a consultation with Fabian, her emotional valet, and time before she would be capable of making some overture of condolence. She asked the robot neighbour for the Trent address and this request sent the poor woman out into the street in order to read the house number off the front door. Then she said that she would prefer not to leave a message for Mrs Trent because she would visit her soon.

On one score Martin had been right. He had said that the Victorians could deal with death because they celebrated it, whereas Maureen could only feel embarrassment about Lionel's inconvenient disappearance off the face of the Earth.

CHAPTER SIX

——————————————— ❋ ———————————————

Sunday was Laura and Martin's day of communion, though there was a certain deliberate tension in the distance they placed between themselves just before they got round to their weekly ritual of consummation. Laura often felt more compliant with Martin's interests on Saturday night, or during the week, when her body felt lithe and her belly flat and smooth, but he rarely made love to her at night, which was a time when he pleaded the lethargy of a full stomach and reserved for a solemn daily bowel movement. When she saw the light coming from beneath the toilet door and heard the rustle of a newspaper behind it, Laura would wonder at the careful, even maniacal, regularity of men.

But on Sunday mornings, when her mouth was dry and clamped together and she was struggling with the waking-up process that follows from an unduly long sleep, Martin would move near her and ask in the manner of a considerate Victorian spouse if she felt disposed to receiving his attentions.

So they would sink down together into the bed's fleshy warmths while Martin indulged verbally in the most wickedly sadistic fantasies. Then they would start to kiss and, assured of Laura's agreeableness, Martin would soon get on to the matter of penetration. Once inside, he would hold Laura's long and narrow back and become intensely aware of her. She was categorically beautiful, but strangely passive and he had come to regard her as the gracious witness to the fulfilment of his base desires.

Martin was a pessimist and he dated the conviction of imminent mishap back to schoolboy outings to the countryside, when he had always been the luckless one who stepped in cow shit. Thus his successful wooing of Laura Clark, renowned as a Julie Christie look-alike, had been rated as an achievement at university. But even as he was escorting Laura out of the student bar with a knowing backward glance at his envious cronies, he had felt nervous. This feeling now appeared to be justified, for his trophy had turned into a prop, one whose support he was beginning to wonder if he could stand up without.

Since Dolores's casual mention of her stepdaughter's instalment in Herbert Laud's New York apartment, Martin had been apprehensive about how he might react to Cassiope again. The Riley Infanta had sprung fully armed from her father's head. As a toddler she had peed strategically in the laps of the famous and when she was growing up leading ladies had competed to read her bedtime stories. Now Laura referred to her as 'an appealing little brat', but Martin found Cassiope more exotic, more fate-defying, than that.

The speculations to which he returned when Cassiope came up in conversation were grounded in an incident that had occurred one Sunday afternoon about four, maybe five, years previously. At that time Martin was only an applicant member of Clive's coterie and he had lent the master the manuscript of his novel in the hope of a favourable and influential opinion. After a few weeks, however, his pessimism reduced him to a state that made the thought of Clive's scrutiny unbearable, so he set off for Tolpuddle Square, uninvited, in order to reclaim it.

Cassiope had opened the door to him and, having explained that 'the parents' were away for the day at a christening party in the country (Fabian was then in his first year at university), she volunteered to facilitate the retrieval of whatever it was Martin had come in search of. Her blonde hair was very long then and as she was leading him up the stairs he trod on the hem of the paisley-patterned gentleman's dressing gown girdling her herma-phroditic body. She had looked scornfully at him as she pulled it from underneath his clumsy foot.

Cassiope knew the secrets of her father's sanctum because she alone had unconditional access to him there. Martin tried to be single-minded about his quest, but this room's contents kept crowding in on his ken. The plethora of hardback books lining the walls and the pyramids of packages – among them his own – and other books littering the floor brought him to a Pavlovian pitch of covetous excitement. One corner was occupied by a Santa Claus sack out of which copies of a new American edition of one of Clive's early novels were spilling. To demonstrate her authority, Cassiope picked one of these up and presented it to Martin. He thanked her and she took this as the signal for the commencement of an act which she began by walking over to Clive's desk and pulling out its top drawer.

Gesturing at the neatly labelled manilla envelopes within, she said 'Love letters to my mother. But, of course, he never sent them because they're really written to himself.'

Out came another drawer.

'That's where he keeps his contraceptives. Just look at that!' She flung a packet of rainbow-coloured condoms at Martin and he read the warning on its side: USE BEFORE JANUARY 1969.

'It's not funny having such a sexy Dad when it means that he has to deny my sexuality. I'm nearly twenty, you know, or did you?'

Martin had a feeling that this display of filial revulsion

was a bit rehearsed. He was relieved when she decided it was time for some audience participation and readily accepted a swig from the half-bottle of Glenmorangie that she produced from the back of the love letter drawer. Inspecting its label, Cassiope informed him that her father had intended naming her after some 'ghastly' Gaelic heroine, 'as if what he plumped for in the end wasn't bad enough.'

'But Cassiope is a nice name.'

Martin knew that this was a feeble response. He felt awkward standing here while she was straddling her father's chair in such a way that it was hard for him to avert his eyes from the garterline of her thighs where the knitted socks she was wearing terminated.

However frequently Martin tried to recall it, the precise sequence of their subsequent behaviour was now frustratingly misted over by a self-censoring amnesia. In those days he used to wear an army surplus greatcoat and when Cassiope glided across the room to stand behind him and tug on the back half-belt, he had been grateful for its woolly shielding of the most visibly aroused part of his anatomy. But Cassiope was too scientific to be unaware of his response. When she had moved around to undo his buttons and begun to cleave to him like an enlongated marsupial infant, he was happy to sink to the floor with her and facilitiate the lowering of his zip.

Martin did have a clear and worried recollection of the effusive endearments that had gushed out of him as easily as his semen had while they were screwing amidst Clive's debris. He hoped that she no longer remembered these utterances because in his experience women were inclined to take them far too seriously. Afterwards he had allowed her to lather his torso with sandalwood soap, even though he felt that its pungency was potentially more incriminating than a natural olfactory aftermath. But there had been no need to worry. On his return Laura maintained a tactful distance from him, assuming as she did that his subdued manner was due to Clive's lack of interest in his novel.

Soon afterwards Cassiope was despatched to university and Martin had not seen her on her own since. She left him with recurring erotic expectancies that were especially tingling on Sunday afternoons, but his attempt to recapture the spontaneity of the original slippage with Maureen had floundered in the face of what he presumed to be her rigorous consciousness of sin. She could only enjoy a game if she was sure of the rules and guaranteed the sort of pay-off Martin felt least inclined to oblige her with — public acknowledgment as an important friend.

Then there was the farcical fandango with Helly Branstorm. He had persuaded her to go upstairs with him during the recent Riley party in the hope of finding Clive's study again. Through an embarrassing miscalculation, they had blundered in on Fabian in a room on the floor above it instead. But in retrospect Martin reckoned that he was probably better off. Raising and lowering her darkly etched eyebrows meaningfully, Helly had told him so much about the hydraulic deficiencies of past and present lovers that there would have been a risk of his own castration if he had gone any further with her.

Cassiope's magic had lain in her moral self-sufficiency. Since he considered that he had been as Leda to her swan, the experience had not felt like infidelity. As he pondered this, Martin glanced over at Laura, who was asleep beside him, and wondered if she had ever done anything worth guiltily nostalging about. Probably not, he thought, because she was too given to the golden mean to match his occasional cravings for excess.

While Martin's prick, like imperial jewels on a velvet cushion, rested against one of her sticky buttocks, Laura was thinking about men — arrows one moment and supine flesh the next — with a tender contempt. She wriggled the feet that had clasped his bony hips and moved away from him, swaying slightly with a clitoral comforter between her legs. With sleepy magnaminity, Martin began to rub her back until she gasped and joined him in their bonus slumber. In the beginning Martin had worried about leaving Laura in mid-air, but now he was resigned to her bleak autonomy.

To Laura it seemed that it had always been like this. She tried to remember if it had been different once. It could well be, she thought, that Martin was like those aseasonal tropical plants which flower erratically and unpredictably – capable of being a fiery and more sophisticated lover with other women – but she was not sure if he could act upon his obvious restlessness. Laura gazed at his sleeping face and recalled her bewilderment in the early days when he had had erections in the street because of her. She pushed her nose into his cheek and he opened his eyes.

'You okay?' he said.

She just smiled and for a moment he wondered what it meant. Then, one long arm across her chest, he drifted off again.

Laura's assent to feminism did not go out much beyond a sense that there was some grand reason for some of the disappointments she had experienced in life. To this vague sense Martin frivolously added her aggressive untidiness and her liking for herbal infusions. Laura had never theorized patriarchy and she was nervous of engaging in a discussion of her sexuality with other women – especially born-again women like Helly Branstorm – because of a fear that some awful gap in her psyche might become obvious. In any case, she reasoned that she was an outcast now by virtue of her secluded nine-year-old marriage and her pre-feminist abandonment of her own (her father's) surname.

Laura was aware of the focus among women of her own

generation upon the quality of the sexual act and she thought that her unselfconscious masturbationary reflex (she had been engineering her blissful descents ever since she could remember and certainly long before she met Martin) might seem like the frantic chewings of a starving person eating grass. She felt a relief when Martin reached his peak efficiently and turned to leave her with the warm bulwark of his sleeping body. Indeed, for her, a difficult part of early married life had been the adjustment to a shared bed. Theirs was a companionate love and she looked forward to a time when this dimension might become calmly paramount.

Later that week Martin left for the new Paris across the Atlantic. Laura wandered about the flat naked and ignored the ringing telephone. She emptied all the ashtrays, opened windows and read the blurbs of many books. After two weeks she surprised herself with the realization that she did not miss Martin – though it was really too soon to judge – and was glad he was not there to witness her disappointment when her period arrived, bang on target. She swung a doleful tampon out of herself with such a violent movement that it bruised the wallpaper in the toilet, leaving a bloody smudge that persisted for a long time afterwards as a nasty reminder of thwarted endeavour.

When she was climbing the stairs in the grip of a knotty cramp, Laura remembered her mother's menstrual rite. Each month, when her father was not around, Laura's mother used to pile up her own and Laura's used sanitary towels – there had been a fear that they would have blocked the toilet if just flushed away – and make a bonfire of them in the back garden. Laura had an abiding memory of their furtive assembly and of the acrid, unholy smell of burning blood.

Laura's parents now lived among the gardenly yeomanry

of a huge retirement home called Sussex. In affectionate mockery of her roots, Martin sometimes called Laura his 'huckster's daughter', but she recognized the barb on this sweet nothing. She had grown up as one of the trades people in an unfashionable London suburb where it was observed with some resentment how publicans' wives dressed up to the nines and shopkeepers' children were not sent to local schools. As the local chemist Laura's father had known who was on Valium, or the pill, and he was a watched man. Avoiding any real intimacy with their neighbours, the Clarks had been careful not to flaunt their relative affluence and Laura had been inculcated with the reserve that still characterized her.

Of course, their family enterprise was a genteel one and Père Clark even owned to a professional status, having trained as a pharmacist before coming into his uncle's shop. Shrewdly, he had deflected the threat from shampoo and toilet-paper-retailing supermarkets by expanding the photographic side of his business just at the time when more and more people were beginning to enjoy summer holidays abroad.

For all their prosperity, Laura's parents had been religiously economical, saving Christmas wrapping paper for re-use in the following year and prescribing a maximum height for weekly baths. Memories like this prompted Laura to have a hot and very high bath, and she sang sentimental songs to herself while she was enjoying the echoing clamour of shamelessly free-flowing hot water.

Her hair had grown with the spring and she did not go to have it trimmed. She wore the old clothes in the muted colours that she liked best and she did very little housework. Every three days or so, Martin rang her at New Vision, but he was evasive about his reception in New York and irritatingly relieved to learn of her period, so she became more and more desultory in her conversations with him. She pushed his clothes far back into the wardrobe and cleared the bathroom of his effects. It was an experiment in being alone.

CHAPTER SEVEN

One evening Maureen retired to her bedroom early with a notion about tidying it up. This vague resolution was prompted partly by the realization that Fabian now had to break through a veritable barricade of books and clothes before he could get near her with the morning cup of tea, and partly by a feeling of exclusion engendered by his anti-social immersal in a new project. Someone Fabian knew, a colleague at the college where he taught 'general studies' to scathing art students by day, had written a book about the Bangladeshi community of East London, and specially-commissioned Fabian Kemp photographs were to illustrate it.

Dressed in a soft old American workshirt, and jeans with such an indecently threadbare backside that Maureen had to venture out to the chipper on the nights when fish and chips was supper, Fabian was hard to extricate from the re-ordered bathroom that served as his darkroom. The fact that he had been promised compensation for his expenses but no payment as such outraged Dolores, but there was no point in nagging him to print the photographs he had recently taken of a new Tolpuddle Square baby. Fabian was immovable, stubbornly committed to this labour of love in the knowledge that his physically distant but psychically near father would appreciate the importance of a *succès d'estime*. Maureen endeavoured to be sympathetic but she couldn't help resenting his industry and he was made aware of this when he heard her, in the room above him, making an unnecessarily loud rumpus. She quietened down, however, after about a quarter of an hour and this was because she was at last confronting the contents of Lionel's carrier bag, which she had emptied out over her bed.

The typescript of the novel was very yellow: either the paper had been very old or it had been purloined from some public office. It was extremely short, only about eighty pages long, and she could have read it at one sitting if she had wanted to. Instead she interrupted her study with violent lunges around the room, mating up wayward socks and chucking out sinister bank statements, because it was difficult to stay with.

She found herself reading the story of Deirdre of the Sorrows, a Helen figure in Irish mythology, but she was uncomfortable with this version of a very familiar tale. It was like having to watch a film that was being unfaithful to a too well-known story.

There had been a calendar (so old that it no longer functioned as such) illustrated with scenes from the legend on one wall of her classroom at primary school. The pictures, which were changed each month as a reward for collective good behaviour, were colourful and shiny like the plates in old fairy story books. Deirdre of the wavy golden hair, vermilion lips and poignant grey-pupilled eyes wore medieval-style gowns with low-slung girdles; King Conor had a pointed beard and was escorted by slavishly devoted wolfhounds; while Naoise (Nicha) and his brothers wore short tunics and cloaks, with heavy torcs around their necks and wrists. It was chivalrous, Celtic Twilight stuff.

The Deirdre story Maureen remembered began at a great ale-feast in the house of Felim, who was a story-teller at the court of Conor MacNessa, the mythical king of Ulster and the lord of the élite warriors of the Red Branch. In the course of this booze-up, Felim's wife gave birth to a baby daughter (the poor woman must have regretted having hubby's mates around that evening) and a seer on hand explained to the carousing company that the child would be known as Deirdre, that she would be exquisitely beautiful, and that nothing but sorrow would come of her beauty.

Despite this gloomy prophecy, the king resolved to let the baleful baby live. There and then he had Deirdre given over to the care of Levorcam, a female satirist and royal 'conversation woman', so that she could be reared in isolation until she was of age to become his bedfellow.

Fate unravelled itself as the predictably seductive Deirdre fell in love with Naoise, one of the leading lights in the Red Branch and, literally, the man of her dreams. By facilitating the lovers' first meeting, Levorcam thought that the prophecy might be undermined, but in fact she helped to set it in motion. Deirdre persuaded Naoise to run away with her and after being pursued all over Ireland by a wrathful Conor, they eventually ended up in Scotland. But when a Scottish king took a fancy to Deirdre, they had to move on again, this time to a small island. There a rumour reached them that Conor was ready to forgive them and that they would be welcome back in Ireland. Despite Deirdre's premonitions of doom, they returned to Ulster where, through treachery, Conor had Naoise and his brothers murdered.

For a year Deirdre was in the bed of Conor and during that time she did not sleep, or smile, or take sufficiently of food and drink. In frustration with her lassitude, Conor decided to punish Deirdre by sending her as a concubine to one of his most loyal henchmen. It was when she was being borne away in a chariot to be with this man that she threw herself off and smashed her head against a boulder, splattering her brains and blood all over Ireland.

In Maureen's childhood the legend's primary theme had been that of thwarted young love but, in what she had just read, the real tragedy lay in a temporary erosion of male morale, the beginning of the end (to culminate with the death of Cuchulain in another saga) of an Ulster tribe's hegemony over Ireland. As an Eve/Pandora/Guinevere figure, Deirdre had unnerved a patriarchal society dependent on a crack regiment.

In Lionel's story, Conor MacNessa had emerged as the central character. Brooding on the ramparts of his great fort at Ewan Macha while extracting favourable portents from hackish druids, this pre-Christian JR remained sympathetic even as he was exacting a spiteful revenge for the slights cast upon his adequacy as a lover and his honour as a leader of men. This had been achieved by making a case for Conor as a genuinely paternal lover of Deirdre. There was more than a hint in Lionel's text that he had bestowed his favours on Felim's wife and that this was the reason why he had decided to ignore the nasty prophecy in the first place. Here the mystical Deirdre was a coy and stupidly innocent *femme fatale*. This innocuous heroine disappointed Maureen, but the portrayal of the wisewoman Levorcam was more seriously irritating. She could have been a sort of female Merlin, but instead she was reduced to a doting, dribbling crone, knitting winter woollies and muttering incoherent curses like a pathetic old witch.

Enraged, Maureen seized a dessicated old pen, actually her sugar-stirrer, and began a stream of withering comments. But then she began to feel a little apprehensive, as if Lionel might rise and reproach her from the dead, and she was guiltily relieved that she no longer had to give him her opinion of the book. Nevertheless, she cleared some space and scribbled more notes. This was quite absorbing, even enjoyable, and soon she had abandoned her room-cleansing operation in favour of smug annotations to the fading typescript.

In the following evenings she gave up her diary, which had faltered anyhow after the complex experience of the Tolpuddle Square party, in order to set off again on a voyage into the pre-Christian past. It was Levorcam's predicament that aroused her sympathy, Levorcam whose misfortune it was to live at a time when patriarchy was being confirmed. The power of satire that entitled her to a certain circumspection at Conor's court was waning and her deeper wiles were redundant in a world where the awe-inspiring reproductive capacity of women was being submerged by the surplus-yielding productivity of men. Of course, she was still very useful as a bringer-on of politically expedient abortions, a forecaster of meteorological likelihoods and a counsellor of impotent kings. But she was only allowed to be wise now in relation to things that were no longer taken seriously. Conor MacNessa humoured Levorcam and kept her on as a mascot, a link with the days of Macha of the red tresses after whom his fortress was named. In tutoring Deirdre Levorcam was casting her pearls before a limpid sex object fit only for exchange.

Fabian was pleased that Maureen was suddenly so busy but he thought that she had developed the suspect tranquillity of a drugged person. Were it not for the fact that he was a witness to her chastity, he would have said that Maureen was in love.

Late at night she would stand outside his darkroom until, like a pet hamster, he would poke his head out the door and agree to share some toasted cheese sandwiches and tea. Because of their parallel productivity a pleasurable sense of well-being arose in both of them, and they cemented this platonic intimacy with a little game whereby

Fabian called Maureen Beatrice and she addressed him as Sidney. (Mrs Webb had been one of Fabian's father's great heroines, the model he had tried, without success, to bring to Dolores's emulatory attention.) One night, as Maureen was hugging her knees conspiratorially to her chest and grinning mysteriously, she asked Fabian if he had ever been 'really in love'.

'Why do you ask?' he said, then adding, 'I don't think I've had the sensation I think you mean. The only person I've felt slavishly romantic about is Laura Kershaw, but that's never been to do with sex.'

Maureen sat up abruptly. She did not tell Fabian why she had asked. All she said, and she was afraid she might have sounded a little churlish, was why Laura?

'Because she is beautiful in body and soul, my image of a perfect woman. I can almost feel her gazing into my cradle, or holding me. I want to feed from her.' Fabian said this in a characteristically self-mocking way.

'Ugh, what would your Mammy think if she knew her son entertained such disgustingly archaic notions about ideal women?' Really, Maureen thought, Fabian was just as bad as Roger, who was always implying that strident know-alls like herself were not fit to wear a skirt. Ever since the days when spotty young priests had come to her school to peddle wishy-washy notions of femininity Maureen had been fiercely suspicious of gender-specific virtues.

'Men like you Fabian,' she said, with an admonishing finger, 'if men like you had their way we'd all be flattered into submission.'

Fabian thought this reaction was a bit heavy and he was embarrassed. He had told Maureen about his feelings for Laura in the hope of coaxing some reciprocal confidence out of her, but she was evasive. She answered his too generously vague enquiry about what she was 'up to' with a grumpy mutter about overtime and the need for extra money for summer holidays. After this conversation she became even more secretive and took to rising early in the mornings. At eight o'clock she stuffed her papers under the bed, climbed back under her duvet and pretended to be just waking up when Fabian came in with her tea.

CHAPTER EIGHT

———————————— ✳ ————————————

Laura patrolled the flat with satisfaction. There was a degree of homely order, just last week's newspapers (to be read months later when they were finding their ultimate destiny as bin-liners) and relatively clear surfaces. The suggestion made by an eminent psychiatrist that a psychopath's wife's obsession with clear surfaces might have contributed to her husband's criminal nature had become a standing joke between Laura and Martin. Indeed Laura had decided to have a little supper party because she thought it might jolt her out of the happy squalor of the past weeks.

She had finished making a salad dressing and was about to make one last survey of the living room when the doorbell rang. She went downstairs to admit her first guest, a puffing Dolores who was balancing a bottle of red wine under one arm and a box of apples under the other.

'From France,' she said, pointing at the apples. 'I thought I'd make you a Normandy apple pie for afters.'

Dolores bundled her way into the kitchen, put the unsolicited apples down and tasted Laura's salad dressing quizzically. Laura watched her with amused resignation, for it had long been evident to her that Dolores Riley's telos in life was a state of hyper-activity. If you gave her a bunch of flowers Dolores was pleased, not like Laura on account of their glorious scent, but because she could busy herself with a search for the right vase to put them in. It was not enough for Dolores to administer two households, Clive's milieu and her dispersed family. Her tiled larder at Tolpuddle Square, stocked high with home-made jams, chutneys, jellies and pâtés, would have put a Victorian housekeeper to shame and she insisted on taking over the orchestration of any social occasion to which she was invited. Seeing that, as yet, there was nothing much for her to do, Dolores followed Laura into the living room.

'My goodness,' she exclaimed. 'What on earth have you got that fire on for? It's very warm in here, you know, there's absolutely no need for it.'

As she advanced towards the mock embers glowing from a curiously kitsch appliance, Dolores realized that the heating bar was not on: for some reason Laura had wanted to keep the fake coals burning. With a conciliatory air, Dolores turned towards her hostess and reiterated her opinion that the place looked 'cosy enough' without them.

Laura was embarrassed, even a little offended by Dolores's tact in dealing with her shocking bad taste. She felt compelled to offer some explanation for this hideous relic of 1960s suburbia, which had been a flat-warming hand-me-down from the dowager Mrs Kershaw.

'I keep it on for Martin really,' she said. 'You see he had a sort of joke theory − it's from Freud somewhere − that men had to be sent out to hunt because otherwise there was a danger of them giving vent to an infantile urge to piss on the fire. So the women had to stay at home and mind the hearth because their anatomy made them more reliable fire-keepers.' Regretting that she had let Dolores in on this complicated game, Laura pulled the fire's plug out.

'Well, well,' said Dolores, 'that's a new one on me. Mind you, though, my old Dad used to say that I had a habit of spitting at fires when I was little. Maybe that was another manifestation of penis envy.'

At this Dolores chortled heartily, in the way that always reminded Laura that the verb came from an amalgam of snorting and chuckling. Dolores would enjoy telling Clive this story when she got home.

The room was not ready yet, however, for when Laura caught sight of a bulging box-file behind the door she went off without a word to fetch a step-ladder. Dolores followed and watched her as she manoeuvred it into place underneath the attic opening. She held the ladder steady as Laura ascended clutching the offensive package.

'What's that you're putting away?' she asked, like Laura knew she would. There was no way to avoid satisfying her curiosity.

'Martin's novel, I can't bear to see it lying around.'

Dolores nodded vigorously. 'Quite understandable. It's a filthy habit. I've often thought they should start a new social service for perfectly busy and self-fulfilled human beings who none the less insist on writing them. They could have a kind social worker on duty who would read people's novels for them. It would be an ideal job for Clive's retirement.' At this she chortled again, but then, peering upwards at Laura's efforts, she continued in a harder vein.

'You've no idea what it's like, you know, with people leaping out of our cupboards and producing their horrible manuscripts. When Cassiope was a student every boyfriend she took home turned out to have one.'

'What does Clive do with them?' Laura asked as she reached the ground again.

'Oh, he puts them away somewhere and waits for a couple of months. Then he gives them back and says that they are very interesting, show lots of promise, etc., but that it's very hard to get published these days. He only reads them seriously if he is interested in the person offering.' (Dolores's conversation tended to leap around.) 'Do you know, it took him six months to find Fabian some useful contacts, but he'll do anything for a flattering young woman.'

Now there was a cold note in Dolores's voice and Laura was sorry that she had provoked this spite.

'I'm just glad,' Dolores continued, 'that Fabian doesn't harbour these types in his entourage, if you could call it that, but I'm a bit suspicious of his flatmate that way.'

Laura was tempted to ask if Dolores's suspicions were provoked by the fact that Maureen was a young (though hardly flattering?) woman, but instead she lightened the conversation by promising Dolores an opportunity of vetting Maureen in the evening ahead. For the first time it occurred to her that her guests, randomly invited that morning, might be incompatible.

Maureen was walking slowly towards Laura's flat. It was as though her focus on the real world had become blurred and she was gripped by a disease with hypochondriacal symptoms – a vague feeling of ill-will informed by a faint but persistent headache. It was always like this when her preoccupation escaped her, thinking about it was like trying to retrieve the memory of a dream.

Generally she succeeded in marshalling it in the mornings. First she fought for a seat on the train, sometimes being unscrupulous enough to unbutton her jacket and jut her stomach forward in a suggestive manner in order to ensure this. Once seated, she could begin to concentrate, to daydream the scenarios that were recorded, at first surreptitiously at New Vision and then more carefully in the late evenings and early mornings.

That morning she had been too tired to wake up early and she had scuttled like a fiddler crab down the entire length of the smelly Tube platform, only to meet the horribly friendly eye of a colleague who had spent the night with an occasional lover who lived in the vicinity. Maureen had felt trapped and resentful. Her precious self-indulgent creative impulses, as opposed to the merely clerical chore of writing things out, had been dissipated by companionable chat. Now she was undergoing a frantic retrieval operation *en route* for Laura's place.

She knew that she was dealing with a pastoral patriarchal society dominated by an ale-drinking warrior élite. They loved feasting and quarrelling, praising and boasting, personal adornment and bright colours. Before battle the warriors stiffened their hair with lime into Mohican quills. With their high stature, weird cries, blaring horns and flashing torcs they terrified the Roman legionaries who met them in Continental campaigns and who were quick to note the expertise of the *gaestatae* − spear-throwers who made human kebabs out of their opponents.

But Maureen was not troubling herself unduly with a strict attention to historical detail, and a necessarily Malory-esque concoction was brewing in her head. She was insisting on room for manoeuvre with gorgeous wine-drinking Rome and the smell of cattle did not have to penetrate the halls of Ewan Macha too overpoweringly. But she was still troubled by the character of Deirdre. This tragic heroine had never been a candidate for Maureen's daily fantasies because she was too much of a victim, and she was blonde. Maureen's feelings about Deirdre's blondness were probably similar to those of a tactful mother who has been constrained to admire the crude make-up of an adolescent daughter. Blonde heroines were too Disneyish somehow, apart from all the other connotations. To give flesh to a Deirdre worthy of Levorcam's care, and creative rehabilitation, Maureen was drawn towards Laura, as yet the only white-haired hetaira she had encountered.

Maureen was the last guest to arrive. Already, Vanessa and the two women from the flat downstairs were reclining on a corduroy couch, while Dolores, up to her elbows in flour, was bellowing contributions to the conversation from the kitchen. Shyly, Laura was dispensing wine in the innocently generous way of people who do not drink very much or very often themselves. She was especially beautiful on this evening. There was an Ingresque creaminess to her skin and a yellow silk dress clung to her body, which had the rounded slenderness of a porcelain figurine. Having settled Maureen in, she sat down herself and observed her guests.

Mona and Liz worked locally as social workers and they had lived downstairs for the previous eighteen months. In their efficient little flat they maintained all the comforts of middle-class childhood. There were regular exchanges of 'pressies', and when they studied summer holiday bro-chures on long winter evenings they had 'bickies' with their cocoa. They were serious and imaginative consumers, always alert to the latest health fad, and their address books bulged with chiropractors and acupuncturists, fortune tellers and healers. Occasionally, they hosted big parties at which Martin had to suffer what he called 'acronymic babble', intense conversations about the short-comings of the DHSS, the CHC or the CRR. But Laura respected Liz and Mona's political seriousness and she found their indifference to review pages and literary gossip refreshing.

The nasal crooning of the old Bob Dylan album, which Vanessa had put on (for want of anything better), ushered in a discussion of his attitude to women. Rather earnestly, Liz expressed the hope that his sexist lyrics were meant to be ironic, but Mona said that Liz was being far too charitable. Laura gazed at Mona, and Maureen was watching her. Laura had never thought about music in this way and she remained uncertain about whether she should be grateful for, or dismayed by, Mona's perception. Martin loved this record and together with the smell of hashish it brought back memories of their student days. Mona's remarks had poisoned this nostalgic package because it made Laura wonder if perhaps she had been, and continued to be, some kind of serviceable and *sympathique*

Dylanesque madonna. She looked over at the dead fire, which was now providing Maureen with a seat, and smiled at herself.

Liz began to tell them what had happened to her that morning when she had been alone in her flat. At about midday the doorbell had rung and she had opened the door to face a disraught woman of her own age. The woman on the doorstep had left her new baby with a childminder for the first time on that morning and now, desperate to be relieved of the milk accruing in her painful breasts, she had forgotten the minder's address. Liz had spent an hour traipsing up and down the road until, finally, they had located the baby.

This story prompted tales of gynaecological adventures. There was the tampon that sailed up far inside Vanessa and the headaches that had assailed Mona when she was on the pill. Dolores contributed an Italian backstreet abortion, which her ambitious first husband had paid for and which had persuaded her to conceive Fabian immediately after-wards. As she talked to them from the kitchen doorway, Dolores punctuated her story with flourishes of Laura's rolling pin, so that she looked like the strong sickle-wielding women of socialist realist sculpture. There was a silence after her story until Maureen, so far pleased with her self-restraint in this conversation, asked the others if they wanted children.

Mona was emphatically against the idea and she made a rhetorical declaration in favour of sterilization and com-munal responsibility for children, but Liz was interested. She told them that she intended to have a baby as soon as she was in her job long enough to qualify for full maternity rights. Laura started to speak, but then she stopped, recalling that powerful moment several months earlier when all considerations of propriety and practicability had been cast aside as she gazed into the pool-like eyes of a cousin's new-born baby.

Luckily, Vanessa had interrupted Laura so her faltering had not been noticed. A Hollywood temptress in her heavy Egyptian-style jewellery, she declared that babies were 'okay', but families were 'terrible'. Everyone applauded this remark and Laura commented that this was her dilemma, wanting a child but not the concomitant nuclear family.

'What does Martin feel?' Maureen was eaten up with curiosity about the Kershaw dialogue on this topic.

'He's not very enthusiastic,' Laura grinned. 'He thinks that I would be a neurotic mother and he is not keen enough on the idea of fatherhood to be more than financially supportive – at best.'

Vanessa popped peanuts between her coral lips and suggested that Laura should ignore Martin and go ahead and have one without his approval. Liz nodded agreement, 'We'd all help you, even Mona loves babies for short intervals.' Mona laughed, but Dolores looked solemn. She went back into the kitchen to check the meal, shaking her head at Laura as she passed and warning her, 'Don't mind them, that's what they all say. There's nothing romantic about motherhood.'

First they had lasagne with a great, violently tossed green salad and then they negotiated Dolores's apple pie. Maureen was roused by this dessert and as she licked her sugary fingers she spoke of its significance for the gathering.

'Remember,' she said, 'Eve tempted Adam with an apple and it was the apple of discord that sparked off the Trojan war.'

Vanessa shifted uneasily in her seat. She had been enjoying the evening so far and now Maureen was starting the kind of conversation she was intimidated by.

'The garden of Eden never seemed like much to me,' was Laura's response, 'because my grandparents had a sort of orchard in their back garden.' This reminded Maureen of

Martin's indifference to the delights of heaven. Had they talked about this, she wondered, but not for long because Laura's response encouraged her to continue talking. She told them of how, at her primary school, the Virgin Mary's intercessionary powers had been explained in terms of the poor farmer wishing to offer up his home-grown apples to God.

'So he prays to Mary first, see, and she takes the apples and polishes them with her azure-blue mantle and puts them on a golden plate, so God is pleased and he looks down on the peasant kindly.'

'That's just a metaphor for early capitalism,' Mona said. 'She's a sort of retailer in the sky.'

'Oh no,' said Maureen, a little surprised by her shocked reaction to this analysis. 'She does acknowledge where the apples come from and to whom the real credit for them is due.'

'Well of course,' said Liz as she turned towards the sceptical Mona.

'It's just like Mum wrapping up the children's presents for Dad.'

At this Vanessa felt able to intervene. 'My father,' she insisted, 'used to wrap our presents for Mum.'

While she listened to them Maureen wondered about Lionel's story. Was her involvement as excusable as the benign intervention of the heavenly polisher of pock-marked apples? She did not speak much after this and the conversation became more and more random. There was a vague discussion of prostitution and this led to an even vaguer consideration of the integrity of their own lives. Each of them, except for Dolores who was rarely explicit about her own niche in life, seemed dissatisfied in some way. Maureen thought of all the restless women she had met: women with abandoned research projects, stalled careers and anxieties about their maternal vocations. Only Laura seemed content, and she thought that might be explained by the fact that she was an unreconstructed woman, a kind of female noble savage.

Vanessa rummaged again among the records and when she had got Janis Joplin raunchily cajoling them, she began to dance. Dolores rose up and went off to start the washing up, and Mona and Liz joined Vanessa. Mona put on her hat, lowered her glasses on her nose and began to clown around the room in imitation of Bob Dylan.

'Can you cook, can you sew, can you make flowers grow,' she mouthed peevishly at Laura and Maureen, who were still sprawled on the couch. Laura was smoking a cigarette, something she did rarely and certainly never in Martin's company. But when Liz put on some Viennese waltzes both she and Maureen were prevailed upon to join the dancing. Maureen took her hands as they rose giggling from the couch.

Maureen took the lead in their waltz, having explained that as one of the 'men' in school dancing classes, she could not be led herself. As they whirled, using too big steps, around the room, Maureen found herself thinking about Martin: the cluttered room still suggested his presence.

'Did you have all this stuff before you moved in here,' she asked her surprisingly amenable partner.

'Most of it,' said Laura. 'I used to buy things in junk shops when we lived in Oxford, but I haven't had that kind of time or inclination since I've been at New Vision.'

'Paraphernalia,' Maureen muttered thoughtfully, as if she was totally unaware of Laura, 'paraphernalia is the personal property of little or no value that a woman takes with her into marriage, which is definitely hers and not automatically deemed part of her husband's estate.'

'How interesting,' said Laura, but she was thinking that sometimes Maureen was a little tiresomely interesting, reminding her of Martin with her anecdotes and references, ready for any opening.

When the music stopped Dolores brought in coffee and

Vanessa began to read aloud the juicier entries in the lonely hearts column of a weekly magazine. Mona and Liz were sharing a joint and when Laura accepted it, Maureen followed suit. There was a sleepy atmosphere in the room until Dolores, drying her hands for the umpteenth time that evening, announced that she was about to depart. Vanessa asked her for a lift and immediately dived around the room in search of the clothes she had discarded in the course of the party.

Their departure was the first betrayal and soon afterwards Mona and Liz made their way out. Maureen searched half-heartedly for her shoes until, as she had been hoping, Laura stopped looking for the phone number of a local mini-cab firm. Then she moved with alacrity to the kitchen in order to make them both a final cup of tea.

Massaging her temples, Laura gazed after Maureen and wondered at her lack of will-power. She had not wanted anyone to stay over, but there had been something irresistable about the pressures emanating from Maureen. With forced gentility, she sat at the edge of the couch and sipped her tea. Then, noticing her frown, Maureen offered to massage her headache away. Laura laid her head back and allowed her pain to be coaxed out. She did not respond when Maureen, who was presumably tiring of her head-ache-banishing attentions, lifted up the ends of her hair and lightly kissed her cheek. She did turn her head in the direction of Maureen's massaging mouth, but she had her eyes closed and seemed to be falling asleep. When they went to bed — the same bed because Laura was too dopey to be bothered making up the spare one — sleep came quickly to both of them.

It was still dark when Maureen was awakened by a Laura who had become an undulating, writhing mass on the farthest periphery of the bed. She appeared to be angrily pushing something out and away from herself and Maureen felt like an intruder in the giant's castle, unsure about whether she should make her wakened presence known by assisting Laura on her pilgrim's progress or pretend to be asleep. But Laura got where she wanted without any help, and eventually she gave out an intense sigh and fell back into sleep, one golden arm raised above her head to expose a discreet nest of light brown hair. Maureen was left, lying still but half-awake, until the early morning light crashed into her eyes through the unlined curtains. She began to focus on the room, the very same setting, the same bed even, where she had once slept with Martin.

Maureen had been invited to the flat one weekend to have lunch with Laura and Martin before being briefed on the *Aspidistra* index. After their meal, Laura had left to visit friends and Martin had produced a bottle of vintage brandy that had been bestowed, he said, by Stanley upon an unappreciative Laura. Under his instructions, she gulped down several glassfuls and then she assumed a delightful sensation of irresponsibility, a liberating awareness that the substance had melted whatever moral fibre she thought she possessed.

She could remember running her finger down the length of his nose and his attempts to bite at it like the fox and the gingerbread man.

'You're nice,' he had said in an offensive rather than amusing sleazy voice. She knew that he was trying to convince himself with this voice that it was not really him, Martin Kershaw, who had his hand on her thigh but she smiled at his antics none the less and their kisses became gradually less economical on saliva. Soon they were entangled in a Rodin-like embrace on the corduroy couch and Martin had cast a wild arm in the direction of what Maureen guessed to be the bedroom. Still a little more sober than he was, she rose resolutely and went in there. She removed all of her clothes and got into bed.

She had felt like a patient waiting to be examined by a doctor because he was so long in joining her and the room was chilly. Then he irritated her by folding his clothes too meticulously on the chair beside the bed. But she was determined to persevere and seemingly so was he. She found it frustratingly difficult now to remember exactly what the sex had amounted to, but she could remember that he had been disconcertingly large in bed for a man who seemed frail, sometimes even effete, in everyday life.

While they slept off the brandy he had clung to her like a drowning man clutching at a log and she was oppressed by him. With her toes she had pulled the duvet up over his back and tried to get some sleep. When she awoke, she pushed him away and leapt out of bed. Hastily, she put on her clothes and abandoned him to the unruly bed and the sticky brandy glasses. For three days afterwards she was afflicted by the nemesis of a bout of cystitis and a fear that he would tell Laura, or that she had come back silently and seen them. In retrospect she reckoned that the erotic dallying on the couch had been the best part, that was what she enjoyed because that was what she had controlled.

Now Maureen rubbed her eyes and gazed into Laura's tranquil face. She was filled with the tense glee of a child who has infiltrated the parental bed. Then Laura began to move. She turned her back on Maureen, of whose presence she seemed unaware, and began her rocking again.

Both Laura's hands were now deep in the flannel folds of her nightdress, which was caught between her thighs. Fascinated, Maureen put out an arm and gripped Laura around the waist, and with her free hand she stroked her hair. As she observed the progress of Laura's frantic quest her original feelings of compassion began to be replaced by more selfish, even arousing ones. But she felt unable to exercise them like Laura. When Laura eventually lay dead and soft again, Maureen lay very still for a long time, exulting in what she had just witnessed for the second time in one night. So this was Laura's secret. Was that how she preserved herself from anxiety about Martin?

When Maureen awoke Laura was sitting beside her on the bed in a red towelling dressing-gown.

'Do you want some breakfast?' she asked, adding that Maureen would be late for work.

Maureen nodded agreeably and went to the bathroom. When she emerged and joined Laura in the small kitchen, which had been so scoured and scourged by Dolores that Laura could find nothing, she was wearing Martin's dressing-gown.

For all the apparent ineffectuality of her light movements, Laura was prompt in summoning up breakfast before them. There was fresh orange juice followed by hot croissants and, like Martin, Maureen opted for tea instead of the evilly strong coffee – her only vice – that Laura usually made for herself. She was amused to see Maureen polishing off Martin's exclusive apricot preserve, but wary of her cockiness.

When Maureen began to serenade her tea, extolling it as the steadier of nerves, the refiner of passions (this called for a glance at Laura) and the promoter of civilization Laura responded in favour of coffee, but quite pointedly gazed at the clock. It was evident that through her passionate rap, Maureen was seeking affirmation of some bond that she presumed to exist between them and Laura was resisting this.

People often insisted on some acknowledgment of her, a sign that she had understood things as they did. For example, while she had been the au pair girl of a very proper and prosperous French family, Laura had been the object of the proverbially rascally elder son's attentions. She liked him well enough, but she did not want to sleep with him because, apart from her youth (she was only sixteen), she knew nothing about contraception and neither, it was obvious, did he. One night she let him into her room and they had held one another for a while before she managed to persuade him to leave. In the morning, when she was awakened by the younger children of the family, his shoes were beneath her bed, so the whole household was led to assume that Jean-Claude had been with the promiscuous English trollope all night long – that was his revenge on her. This incident had reinforced the cautious wariness developed during her childhood, and now she was fending off Maureen with a firm courtesy.

Maureen left the flat alone because Laura was having a day's holiday. Though a little disappointed, she was unsurprised by Laura's distant goodbye after her sympathetic witnessing of the sleep-wank and the homely intimacy of their breakfast together. She told herself that Laura simply needed the reassurance of constant re-negotiation and that this explained why she never let anyone away with a durable keepsake: it was always back to square one. Because she trusted this intuition and because she felt that she was getting the measure of a plausible Deirdre in any case, Maureen was able to desist from joining in renewed office gossip about Stanley's protegée.

For her part Laura continued to be mystified by the significance of this new collusion with Maureen, but then she always had trouble crystallizing things. Her impressions of a film, for example, were slow to form, whereas Martin quickly produced his diagnoses and critiques. She left the evening at the back of her mind as yet another immediately unprocessable experience.

CHAPTER NINE

———— ✳ ————

When the window geraniums flowered, Fabian had prophesied, the colour television would come soon after. He
meant Dolores and Clive's colour television, which they
generally left with him when they went to their house in
France for the summer months. And sure enough, one
Friday evening in late May when there was indeed tiny
flower on one of Fabian's geraniums, Maureen's work on
the Deirdre story was interrupted by the sound of voices
from the hall. She ignored them and continued for a while.
The story was now transferred to New Vision stationery
and it was nearly twice its original length. She was looking
out for all the familiars that she knew and she spelled as
familiers in the text, which was a finishing touch to a
labour whose close she was beginning to regret. She had
found it a good deflectional solace against the enigma of
Laura and the older, though still occasionally smarting,
bruise left by Martin. If Maureen had known of Dolores's
feelings about feckless novel-scribblers, she would have
agreed with her but offered the defence that it was less
pernicious than religion and certainly cheaper than psycho-
analysis.

When the voices distracted her again, Maureen went out
to the landing and sat at the top of the stairs like Burne-
Jones's beggar maid. As she had guessed, they belonged to
a breathless Clive and an eager Fabian, the two of whom
were holding an enormous television set whose splayed

legs kept catching in the banisters. Eventually, they decided to take the legs off and then they managed to settle it into its aestival niche in the living room. Clive lit a cigarette and Fabian suggested coffee. Maureen got the mugs out. Clive could not immediately remember where, or if, he had met Maureen before, but Fabian took the precaution of reintroducing them. Maureen looked sullen.

'I suppose more people claim to know you than you really know,' she said in a small flat voice.

'Why yes, I suppose that's very true,' Clive turned towards her and tried to remember if she was Fabian's lover. He sipped his bitter coffee with very evident distaste (this was another privilege noted by Maureen) and too hurriedly suggested that they should have something alcoholic to drink. Fabian, acting more casual about such expenditure than was his wont, volunteered to fetch something from the off-license. Maureen was then left alone with Clive. She felt boring and diffident, as if the Deirdre project had sucked all generosity of spirit and any willingness to commune with other humans out of her.

While they were sharing a few moments of silence, Clive was thinking that she had the manner of a sulking adolescent, but when she started to talk, it all came at him in a rush.

'Fabian told me that you never knew Lionel,' she said, adding when it was apparent from his expression that he had no idea who she was talking about, 'remember, the man who broke one of Dolores's Staffordshire plates?'

'You mean that you've known the culprit all along?' For this Clive put on a solemn voice. 'You should have come forward earlier with this information.'

'You didn't know him,' Maureen insisted, 'but he came to show you something and now he's dead.'

Clive inclined a pious head towards her and felt relief at the sound of Fabian's return. What on earth was she getting at?

Fabian had bought two expensive bottles of red wine. Maureen was happy to help herself to it while he discussed family matters with his stepfather.

'Cass is coming in June, you know,' Clive nudged Fabian. 'You really ought to try and get over then. You, too, my dear.' (He said this at Maureen because he was obviously still unsure about the nature of her relationship with Fabian.) 'She tells us that she has got fatter and it might be true because Martin Kershaw said exactly the same of her when I spoke with him last week.'

'Americans eat more,' said Fabian. 'It must be very difficult for anorexics to survive in that culture.'

Maureen toyed with her glass, the third she had drained too quickly, but her soul had not budged at the mention of Martin. Even so, the wine must have been having some effect because when the legs of Clive's chair rasped horribly on the kitchen tiles as he was rising to leave, she rushed upstairs. She gathered up the typescript, stuffed it into a cardboard folder, and followed Clive out into the street. When he had settled his tubby body into the car, she threw it into his lap.

'There's some holiday reading for you,' she said with a little malice and Fabian, who looked a bit shocked, glared at her. But Clive just smiled and waved gaily at them as he drove off.

As they were walking back into the flat, Maureen knew that Fabian's silence meant that he was angry with her. She wanted to reassure him, to justify herself by telling him that she was only doing a macabre duty by Lionel, but she didn't. Instead she muttered feebly that Clive would never read what she had given him anyhow, though, of course, that was not the point, the reason for Fabian's sense that she had betrayed him.

Fabian was angered by her imposition, not because of a filial concern about Clive's workload, but because it seemed that Maureen had come out with the unwelcome symptoms of the disease which the Riley household had become a reluctant clinic for. By presenting Clive with a 'work' Maureen had breached etiquette in much the same way as a miscreant partygoer might bore an off-duty doctor with an account of her symptoms. Fabian remained broody for the next week and he did not ask what she had given Clive. Maureen adopted an air of misunderstood nobility and this irritated him further. It was a relief when he set off for France himself.

After her party Laura retired into her own world again. With Stanley's permission she began working at home, ghost-writing for an over-committed horticultural luminary whose name had been the bait that drew in international co-publishers for a book about vegetable growing. In the late afternoon of each working day a courier bore her labours off down to the vegetable fountainhead, and then Laura would listen to the messages on her new telephone answering machine. Maureen's nervous little voice was heard frequently, at first thanking her for a lovely supper, next enquiring about the return of some books she had borrowed and then, Laura guessed, trailing off with no message. Laura might have responded to Maureen and other friends, or visited her office more often, if she had not been readying herself for Martin's return.

When he did come back, Martin was in a bad mood. He looked sourly around the flat, which had been imperfectly restored to its status quo, and swore at Flavia (*Aspidistra*'s dogsbody), who had not achieved all that she had promised in his absence. He would not say much about New York: it was as if he wanted Laura to pretend that he had never gone away. She put his humour down to jet-lag, which she had never experienced and therefore supposed to be a condition capable of producing these symptoms.

Her attitude was rather akin to that of a sympathetic man dealing with his lover's period pains.

They did not make love on his first week home, but early one morning in the following week he woke her roughly. She put her arms around his neck and laughed into his face. He had come out of his coma, or whatever it was. He pushed and pulled her nipples, and moaned her name as if he were trying to memorize it. Laura did come into the office that day, for she was gripped by a joyous excitement and feeling positive about her life. This was because Martin had not noticed that she had not put in her cap. Ordinarily Laura might have wondered why he had lapsed in his vigilance because it was Martin who usually fetched the contrivance. But because it was her fertile time, Laura's hopeful mind was not disturbed by such thoughts.

Her colleagues at New Vision assumed that Laura's radiance on that day was due to Stanley's compliments on her prompt completion of the vegetable assignment, and this confirmed their distaste for her unseemly dedication to duty. They were distant in their congratulations because, as Roger had pointed out, it was all too apparent that Laura had now taken higher vows. Looks were exchanged as Stanley escorted her out to lunch and Roger glanced ruefully at his midden of an ashtray, resolving, for the third time that week, to give up smoking. While he persisted with this habit, Stanley would continue to avoid him, like the beautiful young girls who shunned men with bad breath or body odour in commercials. Maureen, of course, used her intermittent taste for nicotine as a reverse strategy. Whenever there was any danger of Stanley's proximity she would root for the packet of stale cigarettes that she kept in her desk's top drawer and wield a fag like an offensive weapon.

Laura did not encourage Stanley's attentions. But since they did not seem to be sexually motivated and they were extremely difficult to deflect, she saw her compliance with his need of a discreet confessor as part of her job. He had once been alcoholic and now he derived pleasure from getting drunk vicariously. This was denied him with Laura, however, since she drank very little and was unmoved by the bottles that he ordered up for their table. Her indifference confirmed her sanctity to Stanley, his feeling that here was a woman who could turn his cash into grace.

Holding one of Laura's delicately chiselled hands in one of his own great paws, Stanley confided in her his hopes, his fears and some of his disappointments. Somewhere, at some stage, he could not think when, Stanley had missed the seminal boat. Perhaps he had missed it because he was too good at fumbling in the greasy till, although that would be a dubiously moral explanation, suggestive of a necessary connection between art and struggle, and none between art and trade. At any rate, the fact of the matter was that Stanley's reputation, his success, was based on an ability to produce relatively cheap and colourful books. Even though New Vision's editors were instructed to keep the ligature in medieval and encyclopedia, its proprietor was renowned as an entrepreneur, not as a Publisher, one who makes known. Stanley had conquered the business columns, but he wanted to figure in the review pages. Still, in Laura's company, he felt renewed, filled with some of his old exuberance and daring. Perhaps the current could yet serve him up with a pathbreaking entrée and maybe Laura could help him ride it.

'The thing is that what you have is no longer as important as what you want,' he explained to her, thinking inwardly about his beautifully restored house, his talisman wife and his well-launched children. 'It's very important for that reason to keep all your appetites, not to get literally fed-up too soon. You've got to stay hungry to get on!'

Though she recoiled from the nakedness of his drive, Laura felt unable to challenge Stanley's insistence on the importance of a vigilant greed. She sometimes thought that Martin's present disorientation was due to a belated realization that his *Aspidistra* achievements did not necessarily amount to a safe and permanent niche within the intellectual jungle. As for Maureen, she was star-gazing while crawling around the thorny undergrowth, and Laura often amused herself by speculating on her chances if she were allowed to stand up. At least, for the moment, her own desire was for something tangible, the age-old (perhaps now archaic?) victory of maternity. This was her profound option, one that Martin and Stanley did not have in the same way and that women like Maureen could hold in reserve.

Laura lent Stanley her sphinx-like profile and listened to his fantasies, and he was pleased. He resolved to give her an office of her own so that he could talk to her like this more often.

Mrs Muriel Trent was looking very well, though her few friends did not tell her so because they were not sure how she would react. In her distress in the immediate aftermath of Lionel's death she had been unable to give her hairdresser the usual instructions and this neglect had resulted in a new rinse that took years from her still freckled face. She was watering her tomato plants when she heard Maureen's knock on the door. As an exercise this was now as pointless as it was masochistic, for she was bound for the land of abundant tomatoes and in any case they brought her out in spots. Still, she was determined to adhere to each one of her little routines right up to the day when the removal men were due.

She was surprised to see a young woman on her doorstep because she had occasionally worried about a presumed absence of this kind of dimension in her son's life. Maureen presented her with a bunch of flowers and offered incoherent condolences. Lionel had hinted that his mother had abandoned religion after the death of his father, and Maureen wished that she knew of some secular formula for these situations.

She was saved from her difficulty by the thuddering reggae emanating from the house next door. Mrs Trent's neighbours were enjoying their weekend tapes and she pulled Maureen into the dark hall with vehement mutters and an air of casual conspiracy. Having persuaded her visitor to be seated at a gingham-clothed kitchen table and apologized for the unsuitability of a sitting room too receptive to 'jungle music', she put on a kettle. Observing Mrs Trent's familiar procedures, Maureen relaxed a little. Milk was poured from a carton into a blue-and-white striped jug, biscuits – custard creams and Garibaldis – were emptied on to a tiered plate from a tin with a Landseer-style spaniel on its lid, and mugs were disdained in favour of china cups and saucers.

With surprising animation, Mrs Trent began to tell her visitor about the wonderful dreams in which she had spoken with Lionel and been given some understanding of the meaning of his departure.

'It was all over in a split second, you know,' she said this to Maureen several times as if the manner of his going overrode the fact of his death.

It was just like a love affair, Maureen was thinking, the way lovers parted mattered more in the end than the fact that they had. She was pleased with this realization because it offered her some comfort in relation to her Martin-wounded pride. Mrs Trent glanced at her brightened face with satisfaction, reassured that her account of her loss was right because it did good for others too.

'I've got one or two little chores to get on with,' she said. 'But you run along upstairs and take some of his books if you like. I've left everything just as it was, you just browse up there and have something of his. I'm sure he would have wanted that. He was mad about books you know.'

'Did he ever write himself?' Maureen asked nervously.

'Not to my knowledge.' Mrs Trent said this with a little giggle and then she added, 'Mind you, I used to think to myself that that would have been a way out for him. I mean, he read so much and he never seemed to get anything out of all that he read. It was just like constipation, I used to think.' She led Maureen to the little room before returning to her garden.

Except for a too neatly made-up bed, Lionel's room was not like a shrine to the departed. Indeed, it was almost morbidly the opposite, like Maureen imagined the *Marie Celeste* to have been. There were shoes and a soiled man's handkerchief underneath the bed, and the ashtray beside it was full of hard little stub ends. Maureen thought of Queen Victoria, who had fresh clothes laid out on Albert's bed for forty years after he died, though this was an unfair association because Mrs Trent did not seem at all neurotic.

She sat down at the table that seemed to have functioned as Lionel's desk and checked its drawer. It was full of carbon copies of job applications, which had the sought-after vacancy pinned to each left-hand corner. They were in chronological order and sometimes the replies completed each dismal record of endeavour. An enormous typewriter of gothic vintage hulked in a corner of the room and placed over this was a letter of application to Golden Sheaf Books, one of New Vision's rivals, which was dated for the day of the Tolpuddle Square party. The letter's earnestness pained Maureen, but then she became alerted to the fact that its typeface was not compatible with that of the novel typescript. Indeed, so far the room had failed to yield up any forensic evidence of creative literary pursuits.

It was, of course, quite possible that his mother's bibliophobia had made Lionel secretive about his literary efforts. Maureen checked his books, and even behind his bookcase. Still nothing seemed relevant to the Deirdre story, though there was, lying on top of the bookcase, a paperback edition of one of Clive's novels. That was the only clue and to keep Mrs Trent happy Maureen decided to take it away with her. As she picked up the novel a plastic blood donor's card fell out of it and for a few moments she was gripped by the poignant realization that, like her, Lionel had belonged to the O group.

As Maureen was taking her leave, Mrs Trent glanced curiously at her a couple of times. This was because the peculiar hybrid accent, which Maureen had affected in order to avoid arousing more of Mrs Trent's remarkably consistent prejudices, still sounded familiar to a woman whose only bedfellow had been crippled by gutteral Irish ts. But she made no comment and told Maureen that she had been lucky to meet her before she left for Jersey. When Maureen reiterated her sympathy, Mrs Trent waved it aside with a remark to the effect that Lionel had been a 'good boy'.

Embarrassment is certainly worse than grief, Maureen thought as she wheeled a black carthorse of a bicycle on to the street. It was a very old machine, which Fabian had appropriated from Tolpuddle Square for use as a spare, and she reckoned that it must have belonged to Dolores in her district nursing days.

Later that week she got a postcard from France, but it wasn't from Fabian.

> A SILK PURSE FROM A SOW'S EAR.
> COME SOON.
> CORDIALEMENT.
> CLIVE.

That was all it said and in a mingled state of trepidation and joy Maureen negotiated some holiday leave from Roger.

CHAPTER TEN

———— * ————

The hard sunlight beating down on the bus from Orange was unbearably hot. Maureen winced as she caught sight of her bleached face in one of its windows and she glanced anxiously down at her eggshell-white, newly-shaved legs. She fingered her French money furtively and hoped that, in the manner of British royalty, she would not have too many occasions of spending it. Roger had allowed her to take this sudden holiday, though only after he had dismissed the Dordogne as a 'middle-class British colony' and a 'Habitat Blackpool'. Maureen had thought it wise to humour Roger's sense of having seen and done everything before, so she had not retaliated by telling him that she was bound for Provence and for Clive Riley's place, a house that had been acquired before the 1960s.

In her excitement Maureen could only isolate two clear factors: first, that the postcard's wording meant that Clive was aware of her hand in the novel's metamorphosis and second, that he was pleased with it. Seduced by such positive considerations, she was endeavouring to flush away certain stubborn scruples. If she declined to acknowledge Lionel and claimed the whole work as her own, it would be as if she were the deliverer of a gift to an appreciative recipient whose gratitude she was not inclined to share with the real donor. Quite plainly, it would be as if the Virgin Mary were to dispense with giving an account to God of the humble peasant apple-grower. But Lionel was dead, nobody else knew of his labours and Clive would almost certainly fail to remember, or successfully interpret, their conversation in Fabian's kitchen. She resolved to wait and see how the land lay.

Only Dolores was there to meet her and her welcome was so perfunctory that Maureen was considering producing her postcard from Clive until she decided that Dolores was simply very used to, and perhaps irked by, Clive's many visitors. Dolores's brisk and stern manner frightened Maureen, so she resurrected the sickly smile of ingratiation that had been tried first, and with the same minimal effect, on a particularly formidable games mistress at school.

She was conducted to a small room and told that there would be some lunch when Clive and Fabian returned from the nearest town, where they were shopping. Then Dolores left her and returned to her work. She sometimes wrote articles about French food for a Sunday colour supplement and on that morning she was battling with a treatise on goat cheeses.

While Maureen was waiting for the return of Clive and Fabian, she explored the house as best she could without disturbing her hostess. It was a corridor-less eighteenth-century farmhouse. The walls were immensely thick and the windows were so high and narrow that it was oppressively dark inside. A great wistaria crept round the solid walls and attempted to get in the windows, like the plants that coiled around the sleeping beauty's castle. There was a sort of terrace at the front, which Dolores was now occupying as an outdoor study, and the small area around the back was planted with the vines – muscats – from which Clive made his wine. For all its monumental historicity, the house lacked no modern comfort and Maureen guessed that this was due to Dolores's success with French artisans. There was a bidet in the bathroom, which made Maureen grimace as she remembered a jokey conflation of bidets with duvets that she herself at first had not understood. ('We've got a new bidet,' says the one. 'Oh,' says the other, 'we prefer blankets.')

She was relieved when Fabian came back and embraced her with some of his old warmth and then she discovered the probable reason for Dolores's off-hand manner. Maureen had unwittingly arrived on the same day that Cassiope was due.

Romantic films are often described as escapist and though Maureen's private fantasies worked in this way, such films were never palliative for her. When she emerged into dingy twilit streets after hours of watching beautiful people experiencing poignant and passionate relationships, and making history, against lush landscapes, she felt more peeved than soothed because her own existence seemed so mean and flat. Here, in the Riley house in France, she imagined herself to be on the threshold of a more technicolour world, charged with a wider range of emotions, complicated and far-flung relationships, and more money. The Rileys and the people they knew lived out denser lives, more, it seemed, about celebration than survival, and Maureen was itching to get into the picture.

Even so, she tried to stay in the background when Cassiope arrived and as she watched her claim her rightful place at her father's summer court, she wished again that she had not come. With an authoritative procedure of her own, Dolores pushed away each attempt Maureen made to help with dinner and though genial and relatively warm in his manner, Clive seemed oblivious to her presence. Cassiope came with presents for Fabian, Clive and Dolores, and Maureen was timidly grateful to be offered a share in the general provision of New York cheesecake.

Cassiope called Dolores Dolly and she chided Clive about his weight while sitting on his lap and cuddling him in a way that Maureen's father would have found disquieting. Cassiope had the greyhound build of her

113

Parisian mother and brightly bleached blonde hair. Low down on her small nose she wore wide-lobed spectacles, with a tint at the lens edges that made you feel privileged peeping in at her violet eyes. With her hands deep in her pockets and pretty teeth protuberant over a full mouth, she spoke with blithe cynicism about the stupidity of her mother's new lover. Maureen gathered that Clive's first wife, with whom Cassiope had been for the previous week, was still quite young.

Affecting the fatigue of the traveller, Maureen went to bed early so that she could leave them with one exclusive family gathering. Sleep evaded her, however, because she was too wound up by the implications of her summons to France and because the voices from the terrace kept claiming her attention. Once she thought she heard Laura's name. Then her thighs were clamped together like hot scissors as she wilfully brought back the memory of the night in the flat and, ineffectually, mimed the most intense moments.

They all breakfasted on the terrace in the morning and Clive, wearing sunglasses that made him look like a homely gangster, chaired a discussion on the day's schedule. Dolores wished to stay at home, preferably on her own, in order to continue her work, so the others decided to climb a nearby hill, which they called a mountain in order to make its ascent seem a mightier prospect.

Fabian drove them to the starting point. He seemed a little distant from them, unduly focused on his duties as a chauffeur. Maureen watched him anxiously as she sat in the front of the car and helped him to map read. Conspiratorial giggles were emitted from the back seat, where Clive and Cassiope were ensconced like a pair of adolescent lovers and this pattern continued when they reached the hill's base. The besotted father-daughter centaur lurched ahead, while Maureen and the still unusually silent, even priest-like Fabian kept a decorous pace behind. Fearing that Fabian's mood could be due to a persistent anger with her, Maureen asked him what he was thinking about.

'Cassiope is involved with Martin Kershaw,' he said after an interval. 'She gets anything she wants and when she is sure she has it, she usually discards it. She expects me to be enthusiastic about her conquest, but I'm afraid I'm not.'

Maureen looked up at the ascending pair and said more decisively than she had intended that Laura would be a lot better off without Martin.

'He's not worthy of her.'

Fabian looked astonished at her response.

'I thought you didn't like Laura, or that at least you were suspicious of her?'

'Ah no,' said Maureen blithely, 'sure I was only interested in Martin because I thought he could help me get a better job.'

Fabian looked at her sharply. She was so brazenly adept at bullying him into remaking history. What was remarkable was not that she usually succeeded, eventually, in fooling him, but that she so easily convinced herself that she had convinced him. Before Maureen's arrival his mother had expressed reservations about his friendship with her. Dolores had likened Fabian to a tree in a dense forest, obligingly letting a shallow-rooted creeper wind round his trunk in search of the light and nutrition that he needed for himself. He could see an element of maternal protectiveness in her warnings, for Dolores imagined that Maureen had rebuffed his overtures as a lover at some early stage in their friendship. Even so, Maureen was a very demanding friend and he was silent as he came to terms with this latest piece of revisionism.

While Fabian worried about his masochism Maureen was happy in the complete, liberating sincerity of her utterances. She wanted to rub her face against the hot rocks about them, even hug Fabian, in the blissful realization that she was free of any passionate interest in Martin.

'Come on,' she said, taking his arm, 'in fact if you want to know what I really think, I think you and Laura are the nicest English wets I know.'

Clive and Cassiope, bestride a rock that they said was like an early racing car in shape, awaited them. In one of its crevices Cassiope saw a dead snake and having poked at it with a stick, she picked it up and put it into her satchel. Maureen was terrified, how did she know it was really dead? Clive laughed at her terror and said that she had an Irish phobia about reptiles. They made amateurish guesses, none wanting to admit total ignorance, about the identities of the butterflies that soared and alighted around them, and climbed some more before settling down for lunch.

As Cassiope and Fabian laid out a feast of olives, cheese, bread, fruit and wine, Maureen gazed down at the surrounding panorama. She was dizzy from the sunny light and the almost cloyingly perfumed air, and she enjoyed a fleeting image of herself as a fainting Spanish gentlewoman crossing the Andes in the time of the Conquistadores. There was something very unfamiliar about this environment, an intensely horticultural farmscape punctuated by strategically-sited and miraculously intact feudal settlements. But then, like Miss Moffatt's spider, Clive sat down beside Maureen. He offered her an olive and followed her glance.

'You are surveying the land of milk and honey,' he said.

'No,' said Maureen. 'There's no milk, no animals. It's all vines, fruit trees and lavender fields. I used to think that the country meant animals, especially cows.'

'You mean,' Clive laughed again, 'that it's not like the plains of Conor's Ulster.'

Maureen felt cornered. As a defensive incantation she silently recited to herself the definition of plagiarism she had read before leaving London: 'one who steals or passes off as his (or her) own the ideas or writings of another.' But surely it was outrageously presumptuous to lay claim to originality any more: nothing new could come out of the exhausted West. Nowadays it was merely a matter of the timing of the recycling of ideas which, inevitably, must have been prefigured in some other work, some other epoch.

In an effort to avert any more conversation on this topic, she launched herself at the food. Clive left her alone as they concentrated on eating, but in her panic Maureen fancied that he had the manner of a magnanimous cuckold about to condone his wife's confession of infidelity. It was when they were winding their way back down the hill that he started again, asking her how she had come by the 'base text'. Maureen was calmed by this tactful term.

'I found it in your house on the evening of your last big party,' thus she began and it was easy to continue.

'I meant to return it sooner or later, but I got involved. I still have the original typescript, though. Someone at the party must have written it.' She knew that she could not go back now. The decision had been made to exclude all mention of Lionel. She was reluctant to dilute the thrill of Clive's undivided attention.

Before he spoke again, Clive looked down at Cassiope, who was running down ahead of them, hand-in-hand with her honorary twin.

'She's not called after a mystic constellation, you know. I named her after the syrupy blackcurrant concoction my first wife took to imbibing when she was pregnant. Poor Chantalle. I made her miserable because she didn't want a baby, but . . . then she made me pretty miserable when she ran off with my best friend. When I started to write about it all I was using the House of Atreus, but that had been used too often, so I found something I thought was more obscure.'

So that was it, the yellow paper and the huge typeface: it must have been about twenty years old. Though still nervous, Maureen felt enormous relief at the discovery that it was Clive, not Lionel, who had sown what she had tried to reap. She nodded gravely as he continued.

'It disappeared after the last burglary at Tolpuddle Square, not because we were visited by literary thieves,' (at this point Clive chuckled) 'but because it happened to be in the handsome, but ludicrously heavy briefcase they used to take some of the real valuables away in. I had kept *Deirdre*, not because I thought it was any good, but because it was a record of how I felt about Chantalle and my responsibility for Cassiope. It didn't bother me in the slightest when the burglars made off with it – I had never shown it to anyone and in fact I used to worry in case Dolores would find it, because she is still a little threatened by my first relationship.'

Clive adjusted his sunglasses and assumed a comically Machiavellian demeanour. With Maureen's permission – and she didn't dare interrupt – he was about to send *Deirdre* to his publisher in London who would be, he assured her, very interested in it.

'Later on,' he said. 'I'll tell you what to ask the bugger for. It's bloody good what you've done with it, especially now that all this matriarchy stuff is preoccupying everyone. Of course, you are the author, no need to worry about *Deirdre*'s sordid genesis, and you can rely on me for a gentlemanly discretion about our agreement.'

What agreement, Maureen was wondering as Cassiope ran back towards them. She filled Clive's tractable arms with some of the flowers she had wrenched from the parched earth and put on a child's voice.

'Now pater dear,' she said, 'you must write to Lancelot and get him to give Martin some teaching at Columbia. He loves young men anyhow and you needn't tell him about my connection.'

'You make me feel like a Borgia pope,' Clive protested, but it was obvious that he was already composing the requisite letter.

'Hello, hello,' unsure if she had got through, Dolores piped loudly down the telephone until she recognized Laura's tentative, polite voice.

'Just ringing to nag you about coming to join us some time. Never mind if Martin can't make it.' This last suggestion was made in order to spare Laura the possible embarrassment of telling what Dolores already knew.

'Actually, Dolores, I'm very busy now. It might not be possible for me until late August. I suppose you've heard about Martin and I.'

Very calmly said and very calmly felt: Laura could not bring herself to feel that upset. Indeed, she was just a little worried about her passive, even relieved, acceptance of the rupture.

'Oh yes,' Dolores answered vaguely, 'I've heard something all right. Our Cassiope is stomping the place at the moment − silly girl.'

Laura was as anxious to avoid Dolores's overweening, and in this case misplaced, sympathy as Dolores was anxious to avoid discussing the state of emotional play between Laura and her husband. She asked Dolores about the weather and her work, and Dolores then spoke of the first non-family guest of the season.

'You know she's written a novel,' she said in a slightly ominous tone of voice.

'Well, doesn't everyone at some point or another?' was Laura's unsatisfactorily mild response. Recently she had re-read a favourite book from her girlhood, Louisa May Alcott's *Good Wives*. Unlike most of her peers, Laura had not identified with the spirited tomboyish Jo. Instead she had been most moved by the experience of vain Amy, who went to Rome and was so awed by the artistic splendours of that capital that she learned the 'difference between talent and genius':

'Never,' she answered with a despondent but decided air. 'Rome took all the vanity out of me; for after seeing the wonders there I felt too insignificant to live, and gave up all my foolish habits in despair.'

'Why should you, with so much energy and talent?'

'That's just why — because talent isn't genius and no amount of energy can make it so. I want to be great or nothing. I won't be a commonplace dauber, so I don't intend to try any more.'

For a few moments Laura was lost in this recollection — she seemed to be continually lost in thought these days — but then she realized that Dolores needed more feedback.

'Really, Dolores, it's just something people have to get out of their systems and Maureen is young. Besides, it might even be quite good.'

'That's the whole point,' Dolores expostulated, ignoring Laura's second point. 'Some people won't let it out and the more hardboiled they are, the more likely they are to end up duping someone.'

'Has she duped Clive then?' Laura was becoming weary at this stage.

'Oh no, he's on the pig's back. His own work hasn't been going too well lately, so this is just what he needs to cheer him up. She's a sound commercial proposition, green eyes and all that blarney. That's what's really making Clive tick.'

Dolores made it sound almost as though Maureen were having an affair with Clive. But that obviously could not be the case, for no great passion could result from an encounter between a seducer and a seductress. Laura guessed that what was really bothering Dolores was the fact that somehow Maureen had become a beneficiary of Clive's blessings without having her application processed by Dolores first. Laura wound up their conversation by pretending that she was expecting another call and promising Dolores that she would re-contact her soon with a view to accepting her invitation to Provence. The phone call had disrupted Laura's psychological preparations for her biennial visit to her parents.

Budingleigh, the one-pub village where Laura's parents lived, was a south-eastward two-hour journey by train from London. Mrs Gregory Clark usually drove to the station in a nearby town to collect her daughter.

Laura's mother completely, even enthusiastically, accepted Martin's absence. If her son-in-law was too busy to accompany Laura, that was all to the good, suggesting as it did that he might after all be the genuine article – a hard-working husband of family-supporting potential. After years of suspicion of Martin – he was not the professional man she had hoped her daughter would meet at university – Mrs Clark had finally mellowed in her attitude to him. Much to Laura's irritation, she declined to enquire after her worldly pursuits, even though Laura had pointedly bombarded her parents with New Vision books and several times used her father as an unpaid horticultural consultant. As she sat back into the car and grinned dutifully at acquaintances of her parents who recognized her, she felt like suggesting to her mother that she should have hired a carnival float in which Laura could have been more visibly positioned, like some primitive effigy, as a sacrifice to family 'togetherness'. But Laura had yet to do anything that would seriously disturb her parents.

On her last visit to Budingleigh Laura had met with an engaging young doctor (the kind of man who would have made a very desirable son-in-law) who was practising in the village. He had informed her with some pride that Budingleigh was faithful to a general southern trend in its harbouring of a relatively high frequency of people belonging to the AB blood group – universal recipients. Here, in this section of the porous chalky sponge, for so long steeped in and still soaking up the wealth of England, was a density of the fair-pigmented, round-headed, blue-eyed and relatively tall descendants of Anglo-Saxon carpet-baggers. There were relatively few Os, he told her, universal donors. These darker-pigmented, long-headed and relatively short folk were to be found more frequently in the Celtic realms and in those parts of industrial Britain where Irish immigrants confused the genes in the nineteenth century. It had been this memorable conversation, and not a needless anxiety about the viability of their offspring, that had prompted Laura's curiosity about Martin's blood group.

When Laura asked after this Doctor Wheeler her mother told her that he had gone to South Africa, adding with defensive emphasis that there were 'lots of opportunities' there for professional young people.

Her father embraced her when she reached the house and she spent her first hour inspecting his fragrant garden. While waiting for the first of the gargantuan meals prepared for a daughter whose adolescent (boarding school) appetite would never be forgotten, she enthused over winter holiday snapshots. After the meal she helped with the dishes and then, true to old routines, she suffered the rebuff of having some of the items she passed to her mother for drying re-immersed in the sudsy sink.

The *déjà-vu* tedium of this filial retreat might have been relieved, or made more tolerable, if Laura's parents had wished away her external identity. When she had first settled into a velvet-upholstered armchair in their living room, which was crowded out by bulky furniture from her childhood home, Laura had been pleased to see a framed photograph on the wall above the fireplace, not of her and Martin as bride and bridegroom, but of the white Rolls Royce her father had hired to take his daughter to the wedding church. But, unfortunately, the selection of this particular image of her nuptials was no true indicator of her parents' feelings. It was in a painfully marked deference to her protracted education and her literary husband that they decided to watch an arts programme, *The Life of Riley*, on the television.

Like a ring-side boxing coach, her mother exhorted, abused and cajoled her father as he twiddled the television set's knobs, and Laura felt oppressively aware of the elaborate dance they had perfected after thirty-five years of daily rehearsals. Since Gregory Clark had answered all of her worldly expectations, his wife was happy to steward the rest of her Mikado's life and she dealt with him as if he were an exotic potentate hedged in by restrictive taboos designed to enhance his status. He could not touch raw food or unclean clothes, unless, of course, he was divesting his own person, and he could not profane the dishes off which he ate by washing them afterwards. Turning the television on, and adjusting the volume of its sound, was one of the few practical functions left to him.

Laura now found herself in front of the screening of a film, which, she could remember, had been shot shortly before Clive and Dolores's last big party. This film was offering a distillation of Helly Branstorm's experiences at Silbury Hill in order to illuminate the inspiration behind her latest show, an 'anti-retinal experience' entitled *Sperm versus Milk*. According to the artist enragée, Silbury, the largest artificial hill in Europe, was still baffling scholars. The construction of this Stone Age monument was estimated to have kept seven hundred men busy for ten years, but why did they build it? The so-called experts could not come up with sensible explanations, Helly told them, because they were incapable of understanding the symbolic power of the great Mother Goddess in pre-patriarchal cultures.

Laura's mother had got out her knitting: she considered it not quite right somehow to be 'idle' while watching television. Once, in an unusually spontaneous outburst of insubordination, Laura had challenged another of her mother's stern beliefs. She queried the notion that no two things could be done well at the same time by citing her mother's ability to knit and nag, knit and sing, knit and gossip, etc.

Now she knew well that her mother was observing her as she was watching Helly, while her father was keeping half an eye on both of them, so she focused on the small screen all the more intently. In a disconcertingly flimsy dress – it looked, and must have been, bitterly cold – Helly mused aloud with a persistently foreign (maybe Dutch?) and discordantly Americanized accent. Her first visit to Silbury had proved to be a pilgrimage of self-discovery, a road to Damascus, which had precipitated a whole new course in her practice as an artist. As she watched Helly scrambling over the site, Laura's mother bit her wool savagely and remarked that Helly could do with losing a bit of weight. Spite like this would never hold Helly back however.

'Here, I feel is the centre of our Great Mother. I want to find comfort and refuge with the Breast/Eye/Womb/Belly rising out of the landscape so naked and vulnerable. I want to be at one with her, to be with her. I gaze at her mound, so exposed and scarred like a vein-streaked breast that has suckled too many uncaring babes. She means something enormous, powerful and painful and I cannot bear to see her place being desecrated. Heed me, hear me Great Mother.'

It was compelling stuff, especially when Helly began to weep at the sight of barbed wire, and Mrs Clark's knitting was seriously arrested. In fact, she had only managed to do three rows since Helly's stream of consciousness began and this was something, given the normal sweatshop pace of her productivity.

Clive Riley chaired the discussion after the film. Looking even more like a gouty squire than ever, he placated the archaeologists who inveighed against 'feminist vandals' and modified Helly's guttural invective by re-presenting her statements as questions. It was a nimble performance, a fitting climax to this series in *The Life of Riley*. Laura was reminded that Martin had once said that if Clive Riley had been around to introduce Luther to the Pope, there would have been no Reformation.

As the final credits came up on the screen, Mrs Clark settled her slippered feet on a leather pouffe and awaited her husband's diagnosis. She herself was a fan of Clive Riley's because, apart from the fact that her son-in-law had once appeared with him in a programme about censorship, he wasn't 'too extreme'. At the same time, she had been privy to information about his past, which made her suspicious.

Had not Gregory's last accountant been a Frenchman who had known Clive Riley, been taught English by him, in his Paris days? He had met the first Mrs Riley, the child bride who perpetually reeked of garlic, who wore sandals in the middle of winter and who declined to wear maternity clothes so that she bulged obscenely out of ordinary ones during the latter stage of her first and only pregnancy. These facts had disturbed Mrs Clark because they hinted at a world devoid of the decorum that had ruled her own life, but her husband was more forthright in his opinions.

'This Branstorm woman,' he said, turning towards Laura and conscious of his tact in refraining from a rider about Helly's excess pounds and hair underarms. 'Can you really say that she is a genuine artist? There's nothing beautiful in what she's done. As I see it, it's a case of the empress being without any clothes.'

Then he laughed and pointed at the window in the direction of his garden. 'I mean to say. I could cart that smelly compost heap into some Mayfair gallery and call it "life" or something.'

'Yes, yes, you could. Why shouldn't you?' Laura was smiling. At least her father made his positions clear.

'Artists like Helly Branstorm are only trying to say that art is what you want it to be. If she wants it to be great *papier maché* mounds and . . .' (here Laura hesitated because she could not say 'pricks' in front of her parents) 'columns, that's art, and some people really enjoy it.'

Her father shook his head and her mother looked doubtful.

'At least it's given us something to talk about,' she offered brightly, and the conversation subsided into an indolent deliberation over whether they were to have tea, or cocoa, or chocolate.

Lame as it was, her intervention on Helly's behalf had surprised Laura, and it would have surprised Martin even more if he had been there to witness it. Though Helly's confidence stemmed in part from her trust in a notional army of like-minded women behind her, Laura rarely acted in a spirit of broad front sisterhood. It was too obvious, she thought, that some women only retreated into female company when they needed to lick their wounds in peace, and when they were recovered they went back to the real fighting among the men. It was therefore a tribute to the re-educational efforts of the Maureens and the Monas when Laura defended Helly Branstorm, though, typically, she still could not bring herself to like Helly's work, saying that she 'found it hard to relate to'.

Martin, on the other hand, was quite explicitly negative about Helly's art, so much so that he seized upon malicious rumours in order to account for her success. Had Laura ever noticed, he had once asked, the extraordinary resemblance between Helly's young son and Clive?

Thoughts like these made Laura's eyes wander towards the telephone. She had Walter's phone number and she knew that Martin was probably back in London and staying with him. She was tempted to ring him and elicit his solidarity, because he alone could be sympathetic without underestimating the 'blood is thicker than water' inhibitions militating against complete mockery of her parents. She could not give in to this temptation, however, because she knew he would only take the opportunity to renew his plea for a sanctioning of his affair with Cassiope. It was perverse, this need he had for her approval, even when, as far as he knew, he was hurting her. Besides, the weekend in Budingleigh was strengthening her resolve not to follow in her mother's footsteps. Mrs Clark was such a good wife and such a bitter, boring woman.

Soon after Laura returned to London Martin did show up for one last half-hearted discussion of 'the relationship'.

'Laura,' he said with breezy insistence almost as soon as he shut the door behind him. 'We've got to talk. I've got to know what you think is happening. This thing with Cassiope is no big deal, but please tell me what you think.'

'There's nothing to talk about,' she said. 'I feel fine, you feel fine. I still care a lot about you but it's probably best if you get on with your life without taking mine into account.'

'It's not that simple and you know it. What about the mortgage? Or your parents?'

Laura snorted. 'Oh, don't worry about them. The whole thing was really their fault. If they hadn't objected so much to us in the first place, we'd never have had to get married, or pretend to be Romeo and Juliet for so long. They'll accept a separation eventually. And I'm perfectly capable of handling that.'

'Laura,' Martin wailed with his face in his hands.

'Martin,' she wailed back mockingly. 'I just don't have the energy for some dramatic bust-up. We've had too many rehearsals, and your going away was the best thing to happen, even though I didn't know it at the time.'

'You've got it all worked out haven't you? I'm the guilty adulterer but you're much more cool about splitting up than I am, much more organized.'

Martin now began to sound more angry than anguished, so Laura retreated from him. Quietly, she began to prepare some supper and while they were eating they began talking again, more practically this time. Martin realized that the preparation of an agenda for their separation was Laura's prerogative. Every now and then he would glance ruefully at some nearby object, a book or a table lamp, and suggest that she keep it, just to test her strength. But she remained businesslike.

'That, my dear,' she said, gesturing grandly and imitating Maureen Ryan's voice, 'is my paraphernalia I'll have you know.' Then she told him what Maureen had told her about the meaning of paraphernalia.

'Jesus Christ,' he laughed. 'That woman manages to spread a little knowledge a very long way.' The fact that he and Laura could still share a joke at Maureen's expense augured well for the future of their friendship.

CHAPTER ELEVEN

———————— ✻ ————————

Maureen picked up a tolerably good suntan and a great deal of gossip about people she had heard of but never met in France. After the day on the hill things had gone more smoothly for the cuckoo's fledgling. Though the *ingénue* in Maureen sometimes alarmed Clive, he decided that this artlessness was just the flip-side of a personality with harder qualities on the other side. His doubts about the constancy of her intelligence were not serious because, apart from what her imaginative re-creation of *Deirdre* had suggested to him, frequent flashes of sharp spontaneity confirmed her as a sound investment. Maureen, he explained to Fabian, was remarkably cunning. By this he meant that she had an instinctive feel for the responses that would satisfy the exigency of the moment, arriving at solutions not through some so-called rational process but through a perfectly wonderful sense of how her immediate interests could be best served.

Once Dolores perceived that Maureen's baptism was a *fait accompli*, she set about being more friendly and after he watched his mother teaching Maureen how to make a *pistou*, Fabian relaxed. Before she left them, Cassiope asked her over to New York and though Maureen was still discomfited by the bronzed brat's appeal for Martin, she had expressed great enthusiasm for the invitation. All in all, she was justified now in considering herself one of the family.

After only a week back home, however, her modest tan began to fade on some parts of her body and peel on others. She studied her peeling nose fretfully before setting off for the Bloomsbury office of Clive's publisher.

Ralph Newman was bearded and of an undeterminate, that is healthy, middle age. There was a hint of a Central European accent to his voice and he displayed gentlemanly virtuosity as he opened doors, fetched chairs and removed her outer garments before allowing Maureen to be seated in his baroque room. She was not comfortable there because on a shelf above his leather-covered desk – the kind of desk over which bare-bottomed blondes in schoolgirl uniforms are splayed in glossy pornographic magazines – there was a nineteenth-century plaster-of-Paris statue of the Virgin Mary. Her painted toes were curled over the writhing head of a serpent and her face was a little like Laura's.

Despite this, Maureen managed to compose herself well enough to extend a newly developed smile, gracious and yet distant, to the sandy-haired and also bearded (Maureen reckoned that his strategy was probably one of flattery by imitation) young editor who sat near the door, holding a Xerox of her typescript and listening intently to all of the unabashedly Marianist Ralph's remarks.

Readily, perhaps too readily, Maureen accepted their polite recommendations for changes and cuts and then she signed all the papers that met with the requirements Clive had outlined to her. After this the young editor left and Ralph performed more gentlemanly stunts before conducting her to the Italian restaurant where he had booked a lunch table for two. On her way there, Maureen tried to remember if she had noticed her escort at the historic Tolpuddle Square party.

To her immense gratification, she was saluted enthusiastically, though briefly because he seemed to be in a rush, by an even leaner, and therefore older-looking, Martin, who was leaving this restaurant just as she and Ralph were entering.

'So you know Kershaw,' Ralph said as he handed a waiter her linen jacket.

'Yes.' This response was guarded and she was going to add that she had worked for Martin when Ralph spoke again.

'Recognition from the others, one's peers, that's what an intellectual needs most.'

She found this remark a bit enigmatic and covered herself against any of its possibly negative implications by telling him that she only knew Martin because his wife worked at New Vision.

'She's there too, is she? Nice woman, I've met her once or twice. Wonder what she'll make of all Kershaw's flowery dedications to her in his books, now that he's run off with the Riley nymphet.'

Then he asked Maureen how Stanley was and ventured the opinion that he had become 'bloody boring since he's been dry'. To her surprise, these remarks aroused a defensive streak in Maureen about Stanley, New Vision and even Martin. Despite this feeling, she nodded knowingly at them, and she was pleased by his acceptance of her knowingness.

Ralph was cheered by her appetite. It was years since he had lunched with a person who did not sift the meal of fat and carbohydrates and he watched her gorging herself enviously. He began to talk demandingly only when she was slowing down over ice-cream.

'What you've really achieved in your novel is a powerfully authentic atmosphere, a sense of another world and relationships hemmed in by tribal parameters.'

Maureen was dithering about whether she should make the ungainly effort to retrieve her napkin, which had slid off her lap and underneath their table, and was now, in all probability, somewhere beneath Ralph's feet. It seemed politic to retrieve the napkin while he was on this topic but, having surmised what she was up to, he set about locating it himself. His fussy chivalry marked him out as a man who had never lost sight of the immobilizing Ruskinite pedestal underneath every woman worthy of his respect. When he had restored the napkin to her, she was tempted to cast it away again, like a toy-expelling baby in a pram, but instead she forced herself to respond.

'Well,' she drawled, 'I can't be sure, who can? I mean that it's all only guesswork informed by my own pre-occupations. It's a violent and a sensuous world . . .' (here she hesitated, not in search of the right words so much as the right approach) 'but things must have been very different when farting was an art.'

Then she giggled and watched anxiously for his reactions. He laughed, and the waiters smiled because he seemed to be enjoying himself. She was relieved to see that he was pleased: it seemed easy, but it was perhaps best to continue in this vein.

Maureen was getting wiser. The truth was that Ralph did not really care for her book and he was relieved to discover that she did not take herself *too* seriously. *Deirdre* was, as far as he was concerned, 'women's fiction' dolled up with a bit of half-absorbed anthropology, a dash of astrology, a hint of herbalism and a great dollop of mythology all wrapped up in unashamedly Kiltartan prose. But so what? She was obviously game for a hype and for some reason, no doubt a good one, she had Clive Riley behind her. It was a dead cert, given all the people who owed Riley favours, himself included. Only last month Clive had interviewed him for *Modes and Moments* under the heading, 'The Acceptable Face of Capitalism: a Publisher for all Seasons'. She was a prickly number, though, and he felt warned by the way she gutted him with her eyes when he ventured a stage Irish 'me darlin' as they were leaving Rossi's.

When she arrived back at New Vision Maureen regretted having told Roger she would be at the dentist that morning. It would have been much better to have hinted instead at a gynaecological consultation because then he would have retreated from making any comments. As it was, she was forced to affect the swollen jaw of a recent dental victim when she wanted to smile broadly and hug Vanessa, who had just announced that it was her intention to take up the place offered to her as a 'mature' student of French literature at university. Only Laura was unsurprised by this announcement, and that was because she had nurtured Vanessa's ambition all along. A great party was planned for the leaving day, which was only two weeks off because Vanessa was availing herself of her holiday entitlement for the other two. Accordingly, a massive card depicting a curvaceous woman in bikini and mortarboard, which triggered off a predictable chain of reactions beginning with Maureen's disgust and ending with Roger's amusement, was circulated for signatures and donations.

When Vanessa's leaving day came Laura was busier than she had expected and the rising and falling cacaphony of voices, so peculiar to office dos, was already audible when she locked the door of her new room and headed down the corridor towards the Swamp Department. She ducked into the Ladies Room before entering into the fray.

Still she had to pinch herself in order to provoke a pang of loss after Martin's departure and even then that sort of sentiment was not forthcoming. She stayed cool and there had been a certain hardness in her resolute disposal of Martin's tomato ketchup, a concoction she had always loathed as much for its glutinously congealed cap as for his way of putting it on everything he ate. Some people, including Dolores, were hinting that Martin would never

133

have gone back to Cassiope had it not been for Laura's anaesthetized response to his turmoil. In her defence she could only say that she retained an unblemished affection for him, whatever he was up to: it seemed perfectly natural to continue knitting him the sweater she had started in February.

But she had not told Martin about the great project gestating inside her. Why disturb his new-found sense of direction, or that destiny in the shape of a seven-stone Lolita who might prove more skilful than she had been in steering him? Besides, Laura was happily possessed by a fierce selfishness and feeling no need of any immediate pact with the semen dispenser. For too long she had wasted her mothering skills on a grown-up man; soon she would have a real baby to look after. When her condition became obvious she would tell Martin that he was going to be a father, biologically at any rate.

In the classical world women were often likened to the fields in which the precious and solely progenitive male seed was sown, but Laura was earth and seed unto herself, it was a latter-day immaculate conception. Her attitude was rather akin to those reported of certain primitive tribeswomen who separated the sexual act from mother-hood and believed that their condition arose as a result of the entry of spirits wishing to be reborn through the bodies of sympathetic women. It was a matter of being in the right frame of mind in the right place at the right time.

Laura sat on the toilet, a sturdy masterpiece that testified to the ongoing hegemony of British ceramics at least, and patted her ever so slightly, to an outsider imperceptibly, rounding abdomen. But her meditations were disturbed when some refugees from Vanessa's do entered the Ladies. Two women had come in to refresh their faces before re-challenging the menfolk of New Vision.

'I do hope Van knows what she's letting herself in for,' was the opening remark of the first voice, that of an

adenoidal Liverpudlian who presided, like some archaic
custodial monster, over the ante-chamber to the accounts
department.

'Well, she's better off away from here, that's all I can
say,' said the other. 'But who'll old Roger have to grope
now, not mad Maureen that's for certain.'

'Oh they'll get someone new for him. Poor Roger, he
hasn't even got Mrs Kershaw anymore.'

Voice number two giggled. 'Aaaw. She's in Ruckster's
clutches. Can't make her out, she's like a nun somehow.'

'Well she suits him 'cos he's got no balls.'

This sent the demoiselles into fits of laughter and there
was much re-checking of be-kohled eyes as a result. Even
after they had gone, Laura waited several more minutes
before emerging from the lavatory.

As Laura walked into the party room a visibly intoxi-
cated Roger was making a presentation speech. Holding
his paper cup of cheap white wine in one hand and a gaily
wrapped parcel in the other, he was turned towards an
anything but mature-looking Vanessa.

'Students are the last aristocrats,' he was saying. 'I'm
sure you will enjoy yourself. I have not been able to afford
the quality of wine I used to enjoy in my university days
since.'

At this he waved his cup and there was a ripple of
laughter, though Maureen's peal had a derisive ring to it.
But he carried on regardless, explaining that he himself had
been a prodigy at primary school, a 'brain' at secondary
school, but mediocre at university.

'At least, since you've left it until now, you cannot have
shared those pretensions and you won't get a shock when
you find yourself among equals or superiors.'

The laughter was more hesitant at this, and there was
much eye contact around the room while he wound up his
speech. But Maureen was touched by Roger's uncharacter-
istic humility and she even regretted not having been very

enthusiastic about him when Ralph Newman had told her that someone of his name had applied for a job at Newman & Grant. She resolved to remedy this if she were re-presented with an opportunity of doing so. In a rush of goodwill she took a knife from Vanessa and busied herself hiving off great chunks of cheesecake for distribution around the room. It was unusually crowded, even for a leaving party, because everyone knew Vanessa, the Swamp Department's emissary to the outside world.

As she handed Stanley a slice, he smiled at her.

'Thank you Ms Ryan,' he said with a deliberately aggressive z to the prefix he deemed appropriate, 'how's the mirish travail with Gerald's text?'

'Oh,' Maureen shrugged and then made an urgent cigarette-cadging gesture at Roger, 'I'm still gilding that fucking decrepit lily!' That, and the cigarette, sent Stanley away, predictably in search of Laura, who was gently congratulating Vanessa.

Although Maureen was getting to know herself better, she was still incapable of acting with restraint in the face of free wine. Having drunk her fill at Ralph Newman's expense, she nevertheless took advantage of New Vision's largesse and one surreptitious glass of Stanley's Perrier water only speeded up a process that was already too well under way. From her seat on the radiator she caught the drift of Laura's perfume and watched her bending over Vanessa like a hospital-opening celebrity chatting up a member of the disabled population.

Stanley was also aware of Laura's scent, which reminded him of the lingering fragrance of private art galleries, but he could not get near her and he wanted to stay away from Maureen, a young woman who was remarkably uncom-fortable to be near. Really, it was all a bit bloody much.

Here he was, providing them all with jobs and allowing them to start parties in office hours and all they could respond with were insulting suggestions about his whole project. If only they knew, Stanley thought grimly, about the enormous file in his office, bulging with respectfully supplicant letters from would-be employees. He could sack the lot of them and then they would learn the hard way how preferable New Vision's order was to the Dickensian exploitativeness of outfits like Newman & Grant. Stanley felt rage at their presumption, their disdain for the cash nexus as they lived off its smelly effluence, and Vanessa's choice bewildered him. Why did she, a competent, attractive and unpretentious young woman, want to become a student when the experience would never form her in the way it had them?

He was scowling and lecturing a young sales manager on the evils of smoking when Laura finally acknowledged him.

'Come and mingle with the tenants, Stanley,' she said as she took his arm and brought him to Vanessa. Dutifully, he kissed Vanessa on her cheek and shook her hand, agreeing vehemently with Laura's suggestion that she would always find work in her vacations at New Vision.

Maureen kept on with her lone watch from the cold radiator. She shifted her body uneasily when she remembered her grandmother's insistence on a causal connection between sitting on radiators and piles, but settled back again when she realized that, of course, heat was the crucial variable in this warning. She wanted to scream out loudly: I AM A SWAN. She was, she was almost sure, and certainly Ralph Newman had implied as much, about to become a princess, to triumph over Roger and all of his ilk.

Her fuzzy mind dwelled lovingly on an elastic inventory of fulfilled desires: contact lenses, a little car, discreet but none the less unmistakable generosity with deserving friends, Martin's jealousy, Laura's esteem and delighted parents. She swam off to the scene of her 'return of successful old girl' lecture to the contemporary pupils of the secondary school she had attended. Just before embarking upon her theme — something like 'the value of hard work' or 'faith in a changing age' — the head nun was commending her anticipated considerations to the awed girls. Maureen was wallowing in this when Vanessa and Laura approached her.

Vanessa, loosened by alcohol and the feeling that her form-filling and secretive days off were already paying dividends in the form of a new identity, was being more physically affectionate than usual. There were tears in her eyes as she persuaded Laura and Maureen to visit her at Southampton in the autumn and as she tottered out of the room on impossibly high heels there was a general sense that the party would soon come to a close.

Holding his unsteady head above the thinning room, Roger observed the swamp women's meeting and gathered into his focus Laura's Botticellian sinuousness, Vanessa's shapely vigour and Maureen's ambiguous gaminity. Roger enjoyed imagining that this was his personal retinue of women and he took the opportunity to set up favourite fantasy number two, the one in which he was the only man left in the world. It took some doing — organizing a scenario where these ladies were cut off in full health from the outside world — and when a snowstorm did not seem plausible enough, he mustered up the aftermath of a disgracefully casual nuclear holocaust to this end.

He looked deep into his battered paper cup and a delicious tremor rippled through his body as he thought about how they would clamour for his sexual services. Such was Roger's confidence in patriarchy that the likelihood of his being more of a victim than a champion in this situation never crossed his mind. Gripped by his waking dream, he walked towards Laura and Maureen, but as if he were rendered inaudible and invisible to them by some all-encompassing opaque dome, they ignored his hopeful presence.

Because she had heard that Martin had re-joined Cassiope in New York, Maureen was hoping that Laura would be more friendly to her. (With each transatlantic phone call, Fabian became less pessimistic about the relationship. Cassiope had declared that Martin was 'dynamite in bed' and was even talking of a white wedding.) Maureen was also anticipating some comment on her dealings with Clive and feeling a little nervous. At the same time she could not repress her optimism about what she was daring to consider a triumph and, to her relief, Laura's smile suggested that this vanity would be allowed. Laura's approval was important, not because she had any Clive-like exterior authority but because she informed the conscience that willed the deed. She was, for Maureen, as much as for Martin, Stanley and even Vanessa, a public resource with a personal touch.

Laura's feelings were not as unambiguous as her expression suggested and Maureen imagined. Only an hour or so earlier she had seen Maureen clawing Stanley and now, as she watched her responding to blandishments like a cat undulating its back to go with the flow of a caress, she, still, could not be sure that she liked her.

'Well,' she said. 'What have you been up to? I heard from Dolores that you all had a nice time in France and that you've written something Clive likes. Isn't that amazing? When I think of all the people I've known who've sought his interest and now you've gone and got it almost casually.' Laura was thinking of Martin here and of an attic-relegated typescript he had, hopefully, forgotten about.

'I'm not sure what it all means,' Maureen began, conscious that she was imitating Laura's tone and now mindful of Roger's proximity. 'It is funny, though, because I always wanted to be thought beautiful more than I wanted to be thought talented or clever.' This was not entirely true, but Maureen did believe it at the time. Being

139

beside Laura made her want to be like Laura and that meant denying the lean and hungry parts of her character.

Laura looked into her shy-sly face and watched as Maureen gulped down more of Stanley's mineral water. Since she was given to setting imponderables aside, and well disposed towards the world in general because of her own pregnant future, she suspended judgment on Maureen's integrity and opted instead for a celebration of her young friend's adaptability. In any case, there was no danger of their friendship becoming tediously demanding because, Laura reckoned, Maureen would always land on her feet.

Emboldened by Laura's look of frank attentiveness, Maureen told her that she, too, had been hearing things. Laura splayed out the fingers on her right hand and examined them thoughtfully before she responded.

'I'm fine, for now at any rate. Really, Dolores is more upset than I am by Cassiope's role. Poor Martin didn't have the nerve to have his affair over here.'

Maureen didn't dare say anything. It was very perplexing, the way Laura sounded sorry for Martin, as if she were still his only ally against the world.

But now Roger was dangerously close, and Stanley, whose invitation to dinner Laura had declined with the plea of a previous engagement, was also hovering about. Fast thinking was in order.

'Quick,' said Laura as she passed Maureen the cup of wine she had been toying with for the previous hours. 'Drink that and then pretend to be very drunk.'

Obligingly, Maureen drank the wine and then, holding the crumpled cup she lurched backwards, into Roger. She laid her head against his chest and in what Laura thought was an almost ludicrously over-slurred voice demanded another drink. Amused, Roger looked enquiringly at Laura, who disappointed him by solemnly suggesting that Maureen had already had 'far too much'. She took

Maureen from his custody and led her to the Ladies, where it became alarmingly obvious that Maureen was in fact very drunk. While she was throwing up in the sink, Laura regained her own composure and went back to the party room to fetch their belongings.

'She'll be all right. She just needs to go home and sleep.' Laura said this with an air of matronly seriousness, thus reassuring a condescendingly concerned Roger who, without regard to his own state, was offering to take Maureen home himself. Then Stanley came over. He took her aside with a mutter about how he knew how to handle 'these things' and Laura was puzzled until she remembered that one of his secretaries had once had a miscarriage in the lavatory.

'Oh, no Stanley, it's nothing like that. Don't you worry,' she laughed and patted his lapel, relishing the irony of his anxiety on Maureen's behalf.

Somehow, Laura managed to get Maureen into a taxi and then, with Fabian's help, into her grimy little bed. This Samaritan task was made all the more arduous by an ungratefully abusive Maureen, who kept fiercely saluting Laura as 'Wanker Kershaw, fucking Wanker Kershaw.'

Early next morning Maureen woke up with a headache and a mouth that felt like the bottom of a bird cage. Ever thoughtful, Fabian had left a jug of water and a couple of aspirin beside the bed. Having availed herself of these remedies, Maureen began to dwell on all the possibly embarrassing things she might have said or done at the party. After an hour or so's painful contemplation there was still no sign of her tea. Righteously, she rose from her bed and went off to find Fabian. But when she walked into his room, she found him and Laura asleep in the bed. They were rather chastely occupying separate sides of the bed, like the innocuous couples illustrated in children's books about how babies are made. Slowly they both opened their eyes and then Fabian smiled at her.

'Now Maureen,' he said. 'You go and make us all a nice cup of tea.'

EPILOGUE

———————— ❋ ————————

More than three seasons later it is a schizophrenic English
May and Fabian Kemp is weeding in the backyard that
passes in his speculator-built street as a garden. Thick
bindweed covers the redbrick walls enclosing a pro-
crustean bed of old telephone directories and the shards of
the discarded lidless teapots of countless previous so-
journers in the house. Fabian finds the bindweed curiously
comforting but though he feels sad, he does nothing to stop
Maureen from ripping it up because she has left the deep
taproots that will ensure its survival. They are clearing up
the garden as part of a general effort to sell Fabian's flat.
He and Laura are buying a whole house together, while
Maureen looks for a place of her own with the help of a
large American advance.

Laura is typing in the tiny kitchen, finishing her third in-
depth interview with Maureen Ryan for a glossy women's
magazine. (Fabian's photographs of a now hennaed
Maureen posed in front of the bindweed have adorned
other such lucrative features.) Laura is a little though not
much plumper and her skin has taken on a slightly deeper
hue. She has been blessed with a very happy and robust
baby, and in Fabian, who cannot sew but who cooks well
and can make flowers grow, she has found what so many
women crave, the perfect wife. She intends returning to
New Vision soon on a part-time basis. Maureen, of course,
has left, though not without having agreed to write a

foreword for *Mythologies of the Swamps*. (A delighted Stanley has taken the view that it was somehow due to his and Laura's perspicacity that the author of *Deirdre* emerged from New Vision's staff.)

This is the time of year when Clive and Dolores usually rouse themselves from their winter torpor to clean their house and settle their affairs before embarking for France. Number 22 is stale from the aftermaths of a succession of parties and Dolores has hired a domestic home helper for a few days. Her helper is not an embarrassingly down-trodden member of the working class, however, but a student who has proved himself to be an unusually thorough cleaner and who is happy to take his lunch breaks with Dolores and Clive in the kitchen.

Though tired, Dolores is irrepressibly cheerful. She remains convinced that the portrait of Nelson Mandela on the kitchen wall has deterred the burglars who have recently struck at an alarming number of their friends at home and abroad, and the used condom that she has just found in Fabian's old room is a happy indicator that the last party at Tolpuddle Square was a good one. When Clive, who has been tidying his study all morning, comes into the kitchen, she directs his attention to a shabby address book lying on the table.

'Just look at that,' she says. 'We thought it went with the briefcase burglars, but David's just found it between the radiator and the wall in the hall.'

Clive is opening the book and laughing gently. 'Poor little Cassiope,' he says. 'She was so worried in case they'd find out she'd lost it at the Beeb, after being paid to do all that research, but none of these buggers would have wanted to appear in that show anyhow.'

Meanwhile, in the Crouch End flat, Martin and Cassiope are trying to feed 'Spring Vegetable Delight' to baby Benedict Kershaw. Martin came back to London to attend his birth (while Fabian and Cassiope went out to dinner) and contrary to many expectations he has proved to be an enthusiastic seasonal father, even sanguine about Cassiope's interest in producing another baby. He is happier in his academic job because it gives him a secure status along with a sabbatical toe in the wider intellectual jungle. Cassiope has dropped several tantalizing hints about the basis of Maureen and Clive's collusion. Once she said, 'Sometime I'll have to ask Dad if he's got any leftovers for you Martin.' But since he now knows that Cassiope's irreverence for her father is only skin-deep, and he himself has many reasons to be grateful for his father-in-common-law's connections, he does not push her. Martin now basks in Dolores's explicit approval, for she is quite triumphant at having acquired the son- and daughter-in-law of her dreams through just two moves on the board, as well as an honorary grandchild whose unorthodox 'family' circumstances she relishes.

Vanessa has done very well, quite brilliantly in fact, in her first year at university. Although she is now a *Guardian* reader, a front page from her old newspaper, the *Daily Mail*, which pictures her as a member of Helly Branstorm's 'rent-a-mob' on a 'Swamp Silbury' outing, adorns the door of her bed-sitting-room. Vanessa finds these forays exhilarating and she is very active in a movement that has hardened into the most important resistance to cruise missiles on British soil. But the Vanessa who wants to take the toys from the boys is still a skilled exponent of the art of being glamorous and wooable. At present she is enjoying a passionate affair with a linguistics lecturer, an enlightened young man who considers her enduring taste for brandies with soda a small price to pay for intimacy with an acquaintance of conspicuous members of the London intelligentsia.

Roger has finally made it to Newman & Grant, where he is doing moderately well although his wife still earns more money. Secretly he hopes, indeed expects, that the bubble of Maureen Ryan's success will burst soon, but in the meantime he regales his weekend guests with accounts of how she once tried to seduce him and of how he supported her when she collapsed in a drunken stupor at a New Vision party.

It looks as if Roger will be disappointed because Cassiope Riley's New York employer is producing a feature film based on Maureen's first book, to be shot in Ireland, and while he and Ralph Newman are encouraging her to give Boudicca the Deirdre treatment next, Clive is busy with the screenplay. The old dog is still teaching Maureen new tricks and recently she acquitted herself well in a special edition of his current television show. Like Clive, she is known by more people than she knows but she has yet to find a Dolores-like keeper and though she scorns Fabian and Laura's partnership as a 'narcissists' club', the fact is that her most valuable friend is no longer so accessible. She now pays an analyst in order to discuss her anxieties and the only reassurance she is capable of deriving from these sessions is that, since sublimation is the basis of Western culture, it's hard if not impossible to combine art with love.